OF SONGS AND SILENCE

TWISTED PAGES
BOOK FIVE

ELLE MADISON

ROBIN D MAHLE

WHISKEY WILLOW

For my munchkin,
Who always wanted to be a mermaid, but probably not quite like this. This book is dark like our souls.

Red sky.

> *There's something bad in the balance.*
> *I'm starin' into the darkness and I like what I see.*
> *There's a thin line*
> *between a sinner and a savior.*
> *Never once did I ever think it would be me.*

— KIANA LEDÉ & CAUTIOUS CLAY

A NOTE FROM THE AUTHORS

Hey awesome readers,

We know that your little OCD souls are being shattered by the lack of symmetry here, with two books for each sister and only one for Melodi. We feel that same pain. But this was the ending our series demanded, and the way Mel's story needed to be told.

So, Of Songs and Silence really is the last book in the Twisted Pages Series. On the bright side, at least we won't be torturing you with any cliffhangers!

Speaking of torture…please mind your mental health and be mindful of the usual Twisted Pages potential triggers. <3

That said, we hope you love MelAri's story as much as we do!

FOREWORD

How do you scream if you don't have a voice?
And who is there to hear you?

PROLOGUE

MELODI

The endless pattern of the waves crashing into the cliffs, then receding, is slowly driving me insane.

It was the backdrop to my childhood, the only sound in the hours I spent alone in my rooms, wondering if my sisters would ever return. These days, the balcony we used to share is the closest I come to them, or to freedom.

I don't dare leave my rooms, not when Mother has ordered me to stay.

So, I am all but drowning in the relentless song of the sea when an unexpected ship sails into view. My breath hitches in my lungs.

Any ship would be unexpected. There are still weeks left until the waters around the isle will be safe to traverse.

But there is no mistaking the black sails of my mother's ship.

It takes everything I have not to sprint down to the docks, unendingly desperate for the sound of my sister's voice—really, any voice other than the terrified squeaks from the maids who leave my food and draw my bath every day. I stay rooted to the spot, though, watching as one by one, the occupants of the ship disembark.

First is Mother, walking with unusually hurried steps, something almost…frantic in her movements. Disturbed, even. It's so at odds with her usual demeanor that it sends tendrils of apprehension trickling down my spine.

Next comes Damian who, in contrast, is even more smug than normal. Dread churns in my gut before the crew even disembarks, before I confirm the suspicion that has been brewing in the back of my mind.

Aika is not on that ship.

This is the longest I've been away from her, and I have lost two sisters already. I might have thought that she had merely stayed behind in Corentin…

But Mother is agitated. And Damian is smug. And I know that something is wrong.

Though I know Mother won't want to see me, I don't think she'll punish me just for meeting her in the foyer. I can't wait any longer than that for answers. So, composing my features, I fly down several sprawling flights of stairs, reaching the entryway just as the front doors are all but hurled from their hinges.

What happened? Where is my sister?

I can't speak the words aloud, and as usual, Mother won't look at me long enough to read them in my expression. I could write them down, but she will ignore that, too.

I turn to Damian, hating that he is my only option, but knowing that he's already examining my features to decipher my thoughts. For all that he harbored a sick fascination with my oldest sister, he has always looked at me with something close to reverence.

Bile creeps up my throat. At the reminder that Zaina is dead. At his unwanted adoration.

All of it.

"Melodi," he greets me, coming to stand far too close.

His serpentine gaze sweeps over my features in a single possessive glance, accurately reading the questions I can't utter aloud. It's an odd contradiction, the way I both need him to understand me and despise that he can.

He looks from me to my mother, a question in the gesture. She shoots him a warning glare, not deigning to acknowledge my presence before she strides furiously from the room.

"Aika stayed behind in Corentin like the traitor that she has become, along with our dear not-so-departed sister."

Traitor? Not departed?

Hope and dread war within me.

What the hell happened in Corentin?

My jaw drops, and Damian brings up a hand to caress my face.

"Don't worry. We're all Mother needs, you and I." He whispers the words in an undertone, his lips warm against my ear.

I suppress a shudder.

My sisters are gone, which means this monster is the closest thing I have to an ally in this place. My only source of information.

3

The only break to the endless solitude that drives me closer to madness each day.

Looking at his perfect features, the cruelty that lurks behind his dark eyes, I wonder if that's better.

Or if it would be better to drown myself in the turbulent sea of my own mind than let Damian offer me a reprieve from it.

CHAPTER ONE

ZAINA

I stand at the bow of the ship, watching the horizon, both waiting for and dreading the moment when the familiar landscape of Isle Delphine comes into view. Logically, I know we are still weeks from that.

But I'm dreading it all the same.

Images flash through my mind of the last time we were on these waters. Damian's bruising grip. Madame's fury. The water closing over my head just before Natia saved us. My only regret is that we hadn't been able to leave sooner. And that Melodi has been abandoned to whatever mercy our *mother* has left.

I can only hope that she isn't suffering for our disobedience—that we have time to get to her before both Madame and Damian lose what's left of their sanity. Neither of them have ever hurt Mel before, at least not in the creative ways we were punished. Still, that doesn't necessarily mean that they won't now.

Water splashes to my left, and I follow the movement

as subtly as I can. The Mayima have been following us for the past few days, their ethereal eyes narrowed in suspicion. They never seemed to care about the ships on this route before, but now they are on high alert.

Flashes of color speed past the ship, like bursts of lightning just beneath the surface of the water. I can't help but scan each body, each set of eyes, cautiously looking for Natia, who has been noticeably absent since she deposited us on the docks in Bondé.

I'm not stupid enough to inquire about her from these sirens, though. Not when she made it clear that it was dangerous for her to help us.

"It's rare to see you without your giant old man shadow," Aika says as she sidles up next to me, her voice yanking me from my thoughts.

Either she's getting better, or I'm slipping. I didn't even sense her coming this time.

She doesn't comment on my trembling hands or the way I have to force myself to stand so close to the edge, and in turn, I don't comment on Remy's absence. I'm glad he isn't with her. His presence is just another thing that sends guilt churning in my stomach. Every time he looks at me, I wonder if we're both remembering the way I let his mother die.

Not that I could have stopped Madame, but I made an active choice not to step in. To risk Queen Katriane rather than Remy or Einar. There were no good choices that day, but practicality matters little when you're the one who loses.

"He's taking his tonic," I finally answer my sister.

It's the only time Einar has been willing to leave my

side since everything happened—when it's time for him to quell his seasickness once again.

"But it's so much more fun to watch him hurl over the side of the deck every five to eight minutes," Aika quips, resting her arms against the railing of the ship.

I roll my eyes at her, thinking of my mountain of a husband, a man whose only weaknesses are me and, apparently, the sea. But there is no room for weakness where we're headed—into the belly of the beast, back to where it all began.

"We should have found a way to leave them." The words are barely audible over the crashing waves against the hull of the ship, but Aika's sigh tells me she hears them anyway.

"So we wouldn't have to listen to your not-so-seafaring husband expelling the contents of his stomach with alarming regularity?" The corner of her lips tug upward. "Because if so, I agree entirely."

I don't bother to acknowledge her jest this time. My thoughts are far too morose for teasing. "Because whatever mercy Madame may or may not have for us will not extend to them."

I know she's thought about it too. About what we're risking and whether or not any of us will survive this. She sighs again, and I feel the full weight of her onyx gaze.

"It's not up to you to decide who has a right to be here, Zai."

I bristle, but she continues before I can respond.

"Besides, if we had left them, they would have just come after us anyway, and then they would have been even more of a target."

7

I glance over at her, weighing her troubled expression against her lighthearted words.

"I'll be sure to comfort myself with that when she tortures them in front of us."

She takes an exasperated breath, casually resting her head in her hand. "I see someone is feeling extra cheerful today."

She isn't wrong, but there isn't much reason for cheer, either. Each mile we grow closer to the island, I grow increasingly aware that we have no plan, no real hope and just over two weeks left to make one. Not that our plan worked out well last time…

"They've probably arrived at the island by now," I finally voice my concern, one I know we share.

We didn't have a choice. Remy had to bury his parents, and we had to wait for the storms to slow down. More than that, we needed to prepare as well as we could to even have a chance—something I'm still not sure we have. It rankles, all the same.

Aika shrugs a slim shoulder, her nonchalance firmly locked back in place. "I mean, we can hope that their ship wrecked and the Mayima ate them."

A small, reluctant smile appears on my lips. "I don't think the Mayima eat people."

"I said we can hope."

The short-lived amusement dies away, and silence descends upon us once more. Worry fills the space between us as I try and fail not to think about every possible thing that could go wrong—all the things that have already happened.

My sister scans the tumultuous sea, the storm brewing in the distance, and I already know what she's thinking.

We got away. Because of Aika, we got away from Madame. We survived.

But at what cost?

CHAPTER TWO

MELODI

*T*he sea is calling me.

More than just the waves, I have begun to hear music. A song that grows stronger, louder with each passing day. It sounds like it's begging me to come closer, to hurl myself into the depths that have only ever represented death to me.

Or perhaps I want to get a closer look at the beautiful Mayima who haunts my dreams each night, the one I have only caught sight of a handful of times.

Sometimes I wonder if he's even real, or just another figment of my imagination. Another bit of proof of my fractured sanity.

Maybe I made him up, formed him from some desperate part of me that misses my sisters so much that I have created someone to fill the lonely, empty hours.

Someone, *anyone* other than Damian.

A knock at the door pulls my attention away just long enough for the melody to fade away again. Already, I mourn its loss, but I clear my expression of any emotion.

I don't need to turn around to see who is at the door. Only one person visits this late at night. Only one person bothers to knock just to enter without waiting for a response. A play at courtesy, at respect for the boundaries he will never truly grant me.

The sound of the door clicking back into place echoes through the caverns of my mind as the lingering scent of blood and whiskey fills the air.

Damian.

He quietly approaches my spot near the window, his breaths steady and even until he's standing right behind me.

"Melodi." He says my name as he exhales, and I resist the urge to shudder.

Calloused hands catch in my red curls, before a knuckle glides along my spine. The night air is already sticky and hot, but it's nothing compared to Damian's scalding breath on my neck.

My stomach churns, and I try to focus on the ocean's song as it recedes into the recesses of my mind.

No, I beg. *Don't leave me alone with him.*

It ignores me, abandoning me to my fate.

Unable to handle the whispers of breath against my skin any longer, I turn to face him. It's not much better. I should be used to this. This cruel future yawning before me in the form of a torturer. Murderer. Sadist.

This is what my mother wants for me. What she has forced on me.

Not that I have once bothered to protest.

"Melodi." Damian says my name again like it is the

oxygen he has been starved of for too long, a beatific smile on his full lips.

His dark hair falls gracefully around the artful lines of his face, his black eyes boring into mine.

It's almost unfair that something so beautiful can be so cruel. Not for the first time, I wonder if there was ever any good in Damian, or if he was born the monster who stands before me now.

Without responding, I lift my hand to wipe away the blood that mars his sharp cheekbone. He leans into my touch, sighing once more as his eyelids flutter closed. Pressing his forehead to mine, he takes a final deep breath, and I allow him the macabre comfort it brings.

Even as it chips away at part of my soul.

I LIE awake waiting for her to come, my fingers slowly dancing along the chain of my necklace, tracing the gentle grooves of the conch shell it holds.

It is the only gift my mother has ever given me—a piece of my father, she said.

I haven't taken it off since that day.

I wonder if he was kinder. Better. Or if he was the same monster she is now, the other half to her twisted soul. Something inside of me holds onto hope that the former is true, even though I should know better.

Hours pass before Mother finally arrives.

Most of the time, she avoids looking in my direction. The few times her gaze lands on me, she looks away with thinly veiled horror, like I am the mirror in which she views her own demented soul, a glimpse of the death she goes through such great lengths to avoid.

But one night out of the year, for reasons I have never been brave enough to ask her about, she comes to my rooms.

I can't decide which is worse. The rest of the year, where she doesn't let slip an ounce of humanity, or this one night where she fuels the lingering ember of hope that she is capable of more than bloodshed and vengeance.

I wish that I was strong enough to tell her to go away, wish that I was strong enough to do anything but stand idly by, waiting for answers she'll never give.

But I am as weak as she says I am, so I lie awake—just as I always do—and wait for her to creep into my room on silent footfalls. She is even more hesitant tonight than she has been in the past.

Is it guilt? Because for all that she has neglected me in my relatively short life, she has never before promised me to a monster. Whatever it is, she stands in the doorway for a fraction of a second longer before crossing the room to my bed.

I feign sleep, though we both know it for the lie it is. It gives her the freedom to settle on the side of my bed, to reach out an icy hand and gently tuck a strand of hair behind my ear.

To whisper in a voice that's barely audible. "You are entirely his."

Damian's?

13

Is this the final nail in my coffin, then? She doesn't usually speak of him with such gentle reverence in her voice.

For the first time since we have played this game, my eyes fly open. I shoot her a look that is half question, half plea.

Tell me why you're here, tonight, every year.

Tell me why you're giving me to Damian.

Tell me anything.

For the barest, briefest fraction of a moment, I see her features, unguarded, in a way I never have before. Her amethyst eyes are widened in sadness, her full lips tilted down at the corners with something that goes far beyond grief.

No sooner have I glimpsed the expression than it disappears. She snatches her hand back, every ounce of warmth bleeding from her face. She is at the doorway in movements faster than I can track, but just as she gets there, she hesitates once more.

"This is for the best, Melodi." Her voice is only half a shade warmer than her features, conveying something I can't begin to translate. "Someday perhaps you'll understand that."

Then she is gone, leaving me with more of the eternal silence she has cursed me with since she took my sisters from me.

My head spins, resignation overtaking me before the gentle hum of the ocean breaches my mind once again.

The song. *My* song. It's returned.

It's louder than before, pulsating with an urgent

rhythm. I can't risk it abandoning me again. Maybe it will be my salvation. Or maybe it's my damnation.

Either way, I find myself finally answering its call.

CHAPTER THREE

MELODI

The closer I get to the beach, the louder the song becomes.

It isn't deafening, though. More all-encompassing, so thick in the air, I can feel the melody gliding against my skin like silk, can taste it dissolving on my tongue like spun sugar.

It tugs at my limbs until I am closer to the water than I have ever dared to get before. Then my feet are submerged.

My sandals sink into the wet sand, and the tips of my nightgown trail in the warm, receding water.

Is this what death sounds like? What it feels like to be lured into that endless void?

And if so, is it really worse than Damian's blood-stained hands caressing my face like he already owns me?

Another wave rolls in, pushing me, prodding me to return with it. Logically, I know I can't swim, but some irrational part of my mind tells me that the sea is my home. That it belongs to me, and I belong to it.

So deeper I go.

Just as the water hits my thighs, the song stops. Silence pours in. The air is empty and still, but for the rhythmic, maddening crashing of the waves.

I am frozen with fear—fear for what Mother will do when her soldiers tell her that I defied her orders to stay away from the water, fear for the way I am losing my own mind a little more each passing day.

Worse than that is the curious, unreasonable sense of grief at the loss of the song that nearly led me to my death.

It's only as I turn on shaking legs to walk toward the back gate of the chateau that I wonder why the one thing I didn't seem to fear was the water itself. I know better than most what lurks in its depths.

I should know enough to be afraid. And I should certainly have known better than to turn my back on the inky, churning sea while I am still standing in its midst.

There is no time to chastise myself when a cold hand wraps around my ankle. My body slams down onto the beach, sand filling my mouth as I'm dragged back into the sea and into the waters below.

Terror, unlike any I have experienced before, wraps its hands around my throat in an ever-tightening grip. I open my mouth, though, of course, no sound comes out. It's oddly silent, the moment that pulls me to my death. Just a small splash, barely audible over the sound of the waves.

Then the water closes over my head.

I struggle, for all the good it will do, limbs flailing against the iron grip that tugs me deeper into the sea. My breath escapes me in a single, precious bubble of air, rising to the surface I suspect I will never see again. I clamp my mouth shut, trying to preserve what little oxygen might be left in me.

"Kane." A deep, angry voice sounds from behind me, but that doesn't make sense.

There can't be voices down here, let alone one that's warm and clear and ungarbled by the sea. My heartbeat thunders in my ears, my lungs already protesting the lack of air.

"What?" a different, closer voice responds. My captor. *Kane?* "You were overthinking it."

"No." It's more a growl than a word, fury truncating in the single syllable. "As usual, you're underthinking it."

Has my mind fabricated male versions of my sisters arguing to accompany me into death? I search for a memory instead, something to hold onto. Zaina's scent of jasmine and cloves, the sound of Aika's fiddle, Rose's pure, melodic laugh.

Tears stab at the back of my eyes. Zaina will blame herself for this, and Aika will blame the rest of the world. They will both lose themselves over a single moment of carelessness on my part.

"Mayima can't drown." This from the closer voice —Kane.

He swims faster now, the currents tugging at my hair and plastering my nightgown against my skin.

"Then why is she terrified?"

A new set of arms wrap around me, massive and solid and warmer than they should be. There is still no air in my lungs, but the panic ebbs away as surely as the tide, even as my body screams for the air my mind knows it won't get.

"She's probably faking it." Kane's voice is fainter now. "You know who her family is."

My mind is fuzzy, black spots filling my vision that are even darker than the sea around us. Just as I open my mouth to finally inhale, to succumb to my fate, another growl sounds.

"Don't you dare," the man bites out. "We're almost there."

I have no choice, I want to snap back. But of course, even if I had air, I would have no voice. So I will meet my death as I have my life.

In silence.

It's the last thought I have before the darkness swallows me whole.

CHAPTER FOUR

MELODI

I awake to the rough feel of stone beneath my back. I'm breathing now, but the air feels... different. Thicker. Richer.

"We should go. He told us to bring her." It's Kane who breaks the brief silence.

"Well, unless he wants us to bring him a corpse, we'll have to figure this out first," the warmer voice intones.

They're talking about me, obviously. Who wants me? Has Mother managed to make enemies of even the Mayima now?

I remember what Kane said earlier.

You know who her family is.

For an unreasonable moment, my fuzzy mind surges with hope that I might not be related to Madame after all. But of course, we are nearly identical. It's infinitely more likely that she's who Kane is referring to.

"Knowing him," Kane mutters, responding to Ari's corpse comment.

A bitter snort sounds. "Go into the village to send a message about the delay."

There is a long, weighted pause. "Fine. I'll bring her back some clothes, too."

The man sighs. "Kane."

"Ari," Kane responds in a mockery of the same warning tone.

Ari.

A name for the second voice.

"Do as you will," Ari says after a beat. "But take Napo."

Whoever Napo is, he doesn't speak up. Perhaps he isn't here. Something like a suction cup pulls from my skin, then there's a light splashing sound that I suspect is Kane leaving.

The air is charged in his absence, the silence, more so.

"You can stop pretending to be asleep now," Ari says.

His voice wraps around me, soothing all the places my body aches from its recent battle with Kane's bruising grip and the sea.

Is this a tonic? Am I drugged?

Blearily, I force my eyes open.

My head is heavy, pounding, and I blink away the distorted image of a cave wall lit only by glowing neon coral and small green plants.

Why is the cave swimming?

I raise a hand in front of my face, but my limbs are slow, like they're moving through…water. Because *I* am underwater.

My lips part, and I expect the water to come rushing in, but it's already there, no more intrusive to my body than the feeling of air when I'm on land. It's not my lungs expanding, though.

I stretch out a hand to run along the skin on my neck. My pulse is beating faster, but that's not what has caught my attention. A gentle vibration accompanies each inhale and I feel the water surging through my throat, filtering and changing. When I exhale, it's the same.

How is this possible?

Either I've been on the receiving end of one of Mother's tonics after all or...I search the small, dim space, less surprised than I should be when my eyes land on *him*.

The Mayima with the perfect face.

His hair is shaved close on the sides, blue-green waves falling to his sharply angled cheekbones and framing the haunting sea green eyes that bore holes into mine with a question, like I am a riddle and he is certain the answer spells death.

At least it's a beautiful hallucination accompanying me into madness.

He arches a dark teal eyebrow, leaning closer to me and slowly dragging his fingers along my bare arm.

My breath hitches in my throat. His skin isn't precisely warm, but it leaves a trail of fire in its wake that crashes through my body the way lava erupts from a particularly volatile volcano, destructive and unrestrained.

My imagination can't have concocted a reaction like this.

Though it should be insignificant, weighed against the impossibility that I didn't drown, that I'm somehow surviving, existing under the waves of the sea, relief crashes over me.

I'm neither crazy, nor nursing some hidden desire to die. The sea *was* calling me.

Did Mother know? She must have. I wouldn't put it past her to hide this just to be cruel, but for the fact that someone ordered my kidnapping.

What other secrets have you kept, Mother, and how will I pay for them this time?

"You're softer than you should be," Ari growls, interrupting my thoughts.

He says it while he's touching my skin, but his words imply something more.

Does he know I see his face in my dreams? That I have counted every last one of his eyelashes and memorized the shape of his full, perfect lips?

Something in his expression, in his weighty silence, almost makes me think that he *does* know. Slowly, he drags his hand up to my collarbone.

My lips part of their own accord. I should move away, but I don't. He's massive, and he moves with the grace of a predator, with strength in every motion. I have no doubt that he is more than skilled with the golden trident that is strapped across his otherwise bare back.

I could never escape him.

I tell myself that's why I stay rooted to the spot, even as I know I don't feel the revulsion from his touch that I do when Damian is near.

Ari freezes for a fraction of a second before he speaks again.

"Not quite Mayima, but not quite human either," he muses.

I don't bother to argue with him because—well, mostly

because I can't. Without my notebook, I have no way to communicate.

I am silenced, just as Mother prefers me to be.

But also because he isn't strictly wrong. The Mayima don't look very different from us, but for their larger size and brightly colored hair and eyes. There are no scales or tails or visible gills. The differences lie in their skills. They're stronger, faster, and, obviously, can breathe underwater.

My hair is bright red and my eyes are violet, both consistent with Mayiman coloring. I am, against all odds, breathing underwater. But I have never been particularly strong, nor fast.

As he said, I am too soft.

Something almost pained flashes across Ari's perfect features, but it's gone before I can read it.

Then his expression hardens, and he pulls back to cross his muscular arms over his broad chest. The gesture makes the winding tattoos on his bicep ripple in a way that is almost sentient, like tentacles writhing across his skin. Even the markings are beautiful, elegant in their intricacy.

A muscle in his jaw clenches, and for the first time, he looks away from me.

"You're not silenced here."

It takes me entirely too long to realize that he is more than perceptive. He is plucking thoughts directly from my mind.

He can hear me.

CHAPTER FIVE

MELODI

a thousand thoughts run through my mind, followed by a thousand more. I wrench my hand from Ari's grasp.

"You can hear my thoughts?" I think the question at him, and he dips his head in assent.

"The way you're shouting, the Mayima three villages over can probably hear your thoughts," he muttered.

I level him with a look, and he arches an eyebrow to show what he thinks of that. But he explains.

"This is the way Mayima communicate. It's not so different from speaking, but instead of sound, it's thoughts. Most people just know how to guard theirs."

Suddenly I feel even more exposed than my thin, floating nightgown accounts for. Is it worse, having no way to communicate, or having him privy to every thought that crosses my mind?

A shudder wracks through me, and I cross my arms over my chest. Whether out of pity or self-preservation, he expounds.

"Think about it like there is a moveable barrier in your mind. Some thoughts can hide in the shadows, they can stay behind the barrier wall that is sealed in front of them. Those are the personal ones you don't want to transmit."

I nod to show I understand, though I'm not sure I do, entirely.

"Other times," he goes on. "You can let the barrier down just a fraction. Just enough for small thoughts to escape. Those are like the whispers of the humans. Quiet enough that only the person next to you can hear."

I take a moment to shield my thoughts, testing a *volume* that just crosses the top of the barrier, like he said.

"Like this?" I try for a whisper.

He tilts his head to the side. "More or less."

I struggle to recall the last time I had to make an effort at anything. Mine has been a life largely free of expectations. Even my sisters have only ever seen me as something to be protected, the baby of the family, the only one who wasn't trained to fight. Before I can try again, Kane comes sauntering back with a smirk etched into his face.

Ari sighs, the sound echoing in the caverns of my mind, sending a shiver down my spine.

"Well you are back in record time," he says, his brows knitting together as he glances around the large man. "Where's Napo?"

"Probably terrorizing the village, still," Kane answers so cheerfully, it's impossible to determine whether he's joking. "One might think you were trying to get rid of me, Cousin."

Cousin?

26

I dart a glance between them, studying the similar slant to their eyes and the width of their noses. The resemblance is there for sure, but there are differences, too.

Where Ari's hair is teal, Kane's is pale pink, the color of strawberry frosting. His eyes are navy, and his shoulders are not quite as broad. The trident peeking behind his shoulders is silver, offsetting the slightly darker shade of his skin.

Kane is beautiful, but not nearly as beautiful as Ari.

"Ouch," Kane says, his features pinching in offense. "Thanks, Kala."

Kala? Is that an insult here?

I immediately slam my barrier shut once again, a bit embarrassed that I let it down so soon after Ari's instruction. Fortunately, Kane moves on quickly.

"I see you're breathing just fine, which shouldn't be possible, but let's not all pretend we don't know who you are." He gives Ari a knowing glance. "I told you she was faking it."

I am used to being talked about as though I'm not in the room. Mother does it. Her guards and servants are not allowed to directly interact with me. But they probably wouldn't, even if they could, since I can't respond in a way they understand.

It doesn't get less frustrating, though, especially here in this one place where I finally have a voice. Especially when he's the one who kidnapped me.

"*She* has a name," I think at him. "And it isn't Kala. I hardly had time to devise schemes between the time I was standing on the shoreline and when you pulled me into the water."

I wouldn't have anyway. I am not my mother, and I never will be. But I don't bother to explain that because if he didn't believe the thoughts he overheard when I was drowning, he sure as stars isn't going to believe me now. Glancing back at me, he tosses—or rather aggressively *floats* a lump of fabric in my direction. I reach out on instinct to grab hold of it, looking at him in question.

"Not then, perhaps," Kane says, crossing his arms over his broad chest. The tattoos on his shoulder and pectoral muscles tighten under the strain. "But our kidnapping victims don't normally stand out by the water at night. I took advantage at the time, but it does seem awfully convenient."

I want to ask how many kidnapping victims they've had, but I'm not certain I want the answer to that question.

"I assumed that's why you lured me there." I think back to the song that had pulled me to the water, how it didn't stop until I hit the shoreline.

"No one lured you—" Kane cuts off, horror dawning on his features.

His entire demeanor alters as he stares at his cousin, Ari giving him a warning look before the former squeezes his eyes shut. I can't help but find it frustrating, this silent exchange, especially when I'm still struggling to keep my thoughts hidden. When I'm still desperate for answers.

Though I'm beginning to suspect Kane doesn't have those either.

But Ari does.

"Well, you won't be needing these now," Kane says, reaching toward the bundle he had given me to take it back. "We'll be taking you back where you belong."

My grip around it tightens, anxiety swimming through my veins. *Back to where I belong? Delphine?*

My pulse quickens, my eyes scanning Ari's sea green gaze for answers to questions I haven't even begun to ask. I should be relieved. My life might not have been perfect, but at least it made sense. I knew who I was.

Now everything is uncertain, unstable, like I'm standing on a bridge while it crumbles beneath me.

I shouldn't want to stay here, least of all with the men who kidnapped me. But wasn't I captive at the chateau, too? Helpless and alone while my sisters were forced to run headfirst into danger night after night, to give away pieces of themselves while nothing was ever asked of me.

Until she promised me to Damian.

I couldn't help anyone there—not myself and not them.

That's not what's keeping me from wanting to return, though. The song that lured me here might be gone, but I have an idea of who it belonged to, now. The same man I saw in my dreams, that I feel an undeniable pull to.

More than a pull, the idea of leaving him is propelling me into a full-blown panic. I'm so unaccustomed to the feeling that I barely recognize it when it comes on. I don't panic, ever. Not when I was trapped alone in my bedroom without so much as a voice to scream. Not when Mother promised my body and my life to a sadist. Not even when I was taken into the sea to begin with.

But it's here now, undeniable and so intense that it's

blinding. Stars line my vision, and if my lungs were still working, they would be struggling to take in air.

Ari steps between his cousin and me, putting a hand on my shoulder in a gesture so reflexive, I'm not even sure he notices it. But Kane certainly does, tracking the movement with narrowed eyes.

"Peace, Kala," Ari says to me before turning to the other Mayima. "We can't take her back now that *he* knows where she is."

A sense of calm trickles through me, either from his words or his hand on my skin. Even if he is still calling me by that word.

"Well, we can't very well take her with us now that—" Kane starts to argue, but Ari shakes his head sharply.

"Maybe you should have thought of that before you took her." Frustration edges his words.

Kane is undeterred. "Maybe I would have if I had been given all of the extremely relevant information."

The two men lock eyes, Ari's expression as immovable as the rocky cliffs below my tower.

"She comes with us."

There is something final in his tone that sends a shiver down my spine. Kane must recognize it too because he dips his head in a small respectful nod. I don't fully understand the dynamic between them, but Kane doesn't challenge him again.

Only when I'm sure I'm staying, when my heartbeat has slowed in my chest and I can think rational thoughts again, do I address the obvious elephant in the room. The mysterious *he* they have mentioned several times now.

"Who is *he*?" I ask.

Another silent exchange passes between them, but this one is less evasive and more...ominous. Ari meets my gaze, his green eyes as turbulent as the stormy seas.

"The King of Mayim."

CHAPTER SIX

AIKA

*T*he days out here pass with agonizing slowness. Between the grief and the plans that go nowhere and the pervasive sense of doom that seems to have infected our ship and all of its passengers, I want to pull every last strand of my hair out.

Slowly, methodically.

Instead, I focus on the card game, something to distract from the mind-numbing circles of our half-arsed plans to overthrow the overlord we call Mother.

Anything to help pull us out of our heads and give us perspective.

And when that doesn't work... I take advantage of Zaina's long pauses between plays to further Pumpkin's training.

Holding up a piece of dried fruit, I gesture toward the Jokithan king, hoping the monkey takes my silent cue.

Pumpkin's tiny orange head tilts in question, and I nod.

He leaps down from my lap, creeping under the table.

A moment later, I see a tiny hand peek over Einar's shoulder, but the giant doesn't notice. Even if Zaina looked up from her cards, she couldn't see the small monkey hiding behind Einar's silvery blond braids, and Remy...Remy doesn't pay attention to much at all these days.

Within moments, my monkey is back in my lap, placing a long, silver chain in my hand. I can't fight the smile that stretches across my mouth. It's the first time we've been successful, me at communicating what I want him to bring, and him at retrieving it without incident.

"Good boy," I whisper, giving Pumpkin his reward.

He chirps happily, drawing the attention of the king. Einar's massive hands shoot up to his neck, and his expression hardens, though there's no real ire to it.

"Give it back," he barks before gagging for the thousandth time.

I laugh, tossing the chain back to him.

"There is an entire ship to annoy," he says on a sigh. "Must you always choose me?"

"It's more fun this way." I shrug.

"Focus, please." Zaina's tone brokers no argument as she tries to get us back on track.

"You're the one holding up the game," I drawl.

"I need time to strategize," she says, irritably shaking her wavy black locks out of her face like her cards will be magically better if she can see them unobstructed.

I tsk and shake my head, propping my feet up in Remy's lap.

"No, Zai. This isn't chess...sometimes you need to be willing to think on your feet."

She narrows her golden eyes and finally lays down a

pair of spades. "Besides, I meant that we should focus on the plan."

Khijhana rests her giant head on my sister's lap, her piercing turquoise eyes looking up at her in concern. It's unnerving how in tune the two of them are, and the connection only seems to increase by the day.

"I think we should revisit the idea of the dragons," I offer, and everyone's heads snap toward me.

It's an argument we've had several times now, and none of us can reach a consensus.

"If they're connected to the royal line, and Madame was after them anyway, maybe we can use them to help us—"

"No," Einar and Remy say at the same time.

Tension thrums through the room and I groan, rubbing my temples.

"I don't disagree with you on principle, A." Zaina's words are a miracle in and of themselves, since it might be the only thing we don't disagree about on principle. "But—"

"Of course, there's a but," I mutter.

"But," she says again, louder this time. "We didn't have time to go back for them, and we certainly don't now, especially when they are unpredictable at best," my sister adds.

"Which means the chalyx might be our only option left," Remy says, running a hand through his chestnut waves.

I try not to act surprised, but it might be the first full sentence he's strung together in days.

Zaina visibly stiffens, her hands freezing in place

where she's stroking the giant cat's striped head, but she doesn't argue.

"Khijhana is the only one we know of that has been able to hurt Madame. We can't discount that," Remy adds a moment later.

Einar moves closer to Zaina, one hand stroking the chalyx's head, and the other wrapping around Zaina's hand.

"He isn't wrong, Zaina. It nearly killed her to stay behind while you were taken last time."

We all know he's talking about more than just the chalyx now, but it's one of many elephants in the room we choose to ignore for the sake of our mutual sanity.

In a quieter tone, Einar adds, "We will all have to take risks if we're to even have a chance at this."

"I know that," Zaina snaps. "I already agreed to let Aika fight, didn't I?"

My brows shoot up to my hairline as I stare at her in disbelief, as my sister casually refers to me like she did the two creatures.

"I'm sorry," I say, crossing my arms and fixing her with a glare. "And here I thought I was a whole arse adult and a queen."

There's a pause before she meets my gaze. "You might be one of those things, little sister."

A soft snort comes from my right, and I turn in time to see a rare smile appear on Remy's features. It warms something inside of me. I resist the urge to climb into his lap and kiss the expression I hadn't realized I'd missed until right now.

Instead, I fire back at Zaina.

ELLE MADISON & ROBIN D MAHLE

"Well, in either case, it doesn't stop me from kicking your arse, *big* sister."

"Regardless," Einar interjects, stopping the sparring before it can begin. "We need an edge, or at the very least, a back-up plan." He directs the last part to my sister, his gaze darting between her and Khijhana.

"Which is why we proposed that the two of you stay on the boat," Zaina declares.

Einar opens his mouth to argue but it's Remy who cuts in, his cinnamon eyes boring into Zaina's.

"No." The word is final.

No explanation. No debate. Just, no.

Something passes between them, an undercurrent like water just before it boils over. To my surprise, it's Zaina who looks away first.

"Fine," she says darkly. "We all go in."

36

CHAPTER SEVEN

MELODI

*T*he king of the entire sea, of all the seas, is the one who wants me.

I rack my brain for what I know of him, but it's very little. The Mayima themselves have a reputation for brutality, and Kane made a joke earlier about the king liking corpses brought to him.

That could have been more of Kane's dark humor, except for the way that both men appeared to be almost... pitying when they told me.

For all that I was relieved to be staying a moment ago, tendrils of fear race up my spine. Is the king interested in me because of whatever weird half Mayima hybrid I am?

Or was I right before? Is this about punishing my mother? I think of her strength, her speed, her predatorial senses. If I am a hybrid, then I suspect I'm not the only one.

Can she breathe underwater, too? Is that how she made enemies here?

A small irrational part of me wonders if he could be

my father. Reaching up, I grab hold of my necklace, my fingers following the grooves. It hardly seems like a gift from a king, but what do I know of Mayiman culture?

"What does he want with me?" I finally come out and ask, even though I doubt I will get an answer, given their reticence on the subject thus far.

Sure enough, Ari stiffens, the muscle in his jaw clenching as he forms his response.

"That's for the king to tell you." Though his tone is neutral to the point of being cold, something that might be remorse flickers in his gaze.

Kane nods reluctantly, and gestures to the bundle in my arms. "Well then, I suppose you should change so we can get going."

Going. Farther away from Delphine.

Though I still can't quell the unreasonable panic about leaving Ari, the realization that I am, instead, leaving the chateau where my sisters will undoubtedly come to find me fills me with an entirely different anxiety.

Belatedly, I slam my mental walls into place—a little too hard, it would appear, because they both wince.

I have no doubt that Zaina and Aika will come for me. Ours is not a bond that either of them would abandon. They will tear the island apart to find me, and the stars only know what Mother will do to them for it.

"I have a condition," I say, lowering my shields enough to get the words out.

"Weren't you just panicking over going home roughly thirty seconds ago?" Kane's mental tone drips with sarcasm while Ari studies me, his jaw still clenching.

Home. Even though I've always referred to the chateau

that way before, the word sounds off now, like a dissonant chord. Brushing that feeling off, I focus on the issue at hand.

"I need to get word to my sisters."

"You're hardly in a position to make demands." Again, Ari's words are factual, but something brims beneath the surface.

"I assumed it would be easier if I cooperated." I'm not posturing.

I *do* assume that.

He studies me for a moment, assessing me the way a predator would their prey.

"Easier, perhaps, but I could always just tie you up and drag you behind us." Ari's tone darkens with each word.

I meet his stare. Something in the grim set of his features tells me he would do it, but I don't think he would particularly enjoy having to be that person for me. For anyone, maybe.

"Is that really who you want to be?" I think the words softly enough that I'm not even sure if he hears me, until his expression goes flat.

"You have no idea the things I am capable of, Kala."

He isn't bluffing. There is a ruthlessness to him, and I don't doubt the things he would do or has done. I see, too, the barest edge of self-loathing that I have often spied on my sisters, something that is noticeably absent from both Mother and Damian.

"Perhaps not," I allow. "But I know cruelty. I know evil. And you are not that."

Whether it's my words or the history they indicate,

something incrementally softens in Ari's gaze. I press my advantage.

"This way, we both get what we want. You, a compliant prisoner, and I, the reassurance that my sisters won't die trying to find me."

His eyes burn into mine.

"You don't have the slightest idea what I want, Kala." There is a long pause, his words suspended in the water between us. "But fine. You have your deal." He turns around, tapping a somewhat stunned Kane to do the same. "Now get dressed. We are behind as it is."

His acquiescence doesn't feel nearly as much like a victory as it should when everything he says leaves me with more questions than answers.

It shouldn't matter.

I am nothing more than his prisoner, even if this strange pull tells me otherwise.

CHAPTER EIGHT

MELODI

*O*nce they've moved a small distance away, I glance down at the materials that are supposed to pass for clothing.

My silk nightdress leaves very little to the imagination the way it's plastered against me to reveal every curve and arch of my body, but the outfit Kane brought is even worse.

Metallic netting has been pieced together with shells and coral and twine in what I assume is a top and skirt. Though that's an exceedingly generous term for the scraps of fabric. I arch an eyebrow at the two males who are silently waiting for me to don fishing tackle.

"Is this missing something?" I can't mask the incredulous tone of my thoughts.

The gowns in Delphine are sleeveless and flowing, but they cover me from neck to toe.

"It's what all of the villagers wear." The muscles in Ari's back grow taut as he raises a hand, presumably to pinch the bridge of his nose.

A huff of water escapes me like a breath and I glance pointedly at his pants—the ones made of solid scaled material, not see-through netting. Even though he can't see me, apparently, my thoughts are enough to give me away.

"These are armor, Kala. For the warriors."

Whereas I'm just a useless woman.

"There are female warriors, too."

I could almost swear there was amusement edging his frustration this time. Briefly, I wonder if the female warriors are given shirts, or if they go topless like these two.

Kane's shoulders shake and Ari hangs his head.

I suppose this is better than the alternative.

Resting my new clothes on a glowing algae covered rock, I try to undo the laces of my nightgown. Of course, that would have been easier if they weren't soaking wet and tangled. It's not enough room to stretch over my head, even if the fabric wasn't sodden and twisted and impossible to wrestle out of.

I tilt my head and observe the two silent Mayima.

"I may need some assistance..." I tentatively...say? That's not quite right since I don't speak, but it feels as good a term as any.

There is a pregnant silence and I wonder if they heard me.

"Can't you just rip the fabric?" Ari asks.

"Don't you think I tried that before asking?" I huff, a bit of my frustration leaking out. Frustration with this situation, this tiny barely there outfit, and my own weakness.

I don't have Mayima strength. I barely have regular human strength.

Ari's fists clench, and he exhales deeply. He spins around, gracefully making his way over to me in a fluid combination of swimming and something closer to walking. His towering form looms over mine and I'm careful to avoid his gaze.

Turning my back to his muscled chest, I pull my hair over one shoulder, trying to brace myself against his touch once again.

He wastes no time in bringing his fingertips to the nape of my neck, his calloused skin contrasting with the silky fabric. Then he cleanly rips the fabric in two, exposing me all the way down.

I can't help the shiver that overtakes me, one that has nothing to do with the cooler temperature of the waters down here.

Ari freezes. Though he hasn't moved closer, the heat suddenly emanating from his skin warms me from the inside out. Does he feel it, too? This thrumming between us, this magnetic pull that has me wanting to lean into his touch.

"Well," Kane drags out the word, startling me from my wandering thoughts. "As much as I'm enjoying being privy to Kala's thoughts and whatever the hell else is going on here, I think I'll go find Napo, and warn him to stay far, far away. Kindly alert me when her shields are back up."

Ari backs away abruptly enough that I question if he was half as caught up in the moment as I was. I slam my mental walls up, as he follows his cousin out of the cave.

Apparently, he also doesn't want to be accosted by my thoughts.

I slide out of my nightgown. While I get dressed, I practice shielding my mind, bringing the walls up, then down.

It takes all of my bravery to glance down my body when I'm finished. As I suspected, the clothes do more to adorn my body than hide it. The fabric is surprisingly secure, though, easy to tie into place and more supportive than I'm expecting.

At least I won't be exposing even more of myself, small comfort that is.

I call to my kidnappers that I am more or less dressed, and they reappear at the mouth of the cave, some kind of strange purple seaweed undulating in their wake.

A flush rises in me as Ari's scrutinizing gaze roams over my body. His massive arms are folded, the sharp lines of his tattoo thrown into contrast by the flickering lights of the sea life around us.

Self-consciously, I tug at the seaweed and netting, wondering if I've put everything on correctly.

"No, it's right," Ari says. "It looks…fine."

"Yes," Kane says with a trace of exasperation. "You look fine. Ari looks fine. I look more than fine. Can we be off now?"

"I—" I hesitate.

Floating here in the cave was one thing, but I haven't had to move much in the water.

Ari blinks in surprise. "You can't swim."

It bothers me more than it should, an echo of my mother's constant refrain.

She can't speak.

I am mute on land. I am weak and incapable here.

Defective everywhere I go.

"The court is going to eat her alive," Kane mutters, running a hand over his face.

"It's fine. She'll learn along the way." Ari's tone leaves no room for argument, not from Kane and not from me.

Again, I feel it, the somewhat heady sensation of being issued a challenge to rise to, a goal to meet, rather than being treated like something weak. He believes I can learn to swim just fine.

More than that, he demands it.

So I nod, even though we both know learning will only get me so far when my stamina won't be close to what theirs is.

What I thought was seaweed moves from the darker depths of the water, startling me from my thoughts. Inky black eyes peer curiously at me from what I now realize is a purple head, surrounded by...tentacles. An octopus.

An enormous one, far bigger than the tiny ones we eat on land.

Kane's face darkens with a rare bit of seriousness. "Best keep that to yourself, Kala."

Can the octopus read my thoughts also?

Ari barks out what might be a laugh before he smothers it with his usual grumpy expression. "No, Kala. But the other Mayima can, and they won't take kindly to it."

The octopus draws closer, and I wonder if I should be concerned, but neither Ari nor Kane seem fazed by its presence.

45

He raises up one tentacle and holds out a stringy length of seaweed. When I don't take it, I am fairly certain that he rolls his eyes at me.

The creature switches his intelligent gaze to glare at Ari in a manner I might call...pointed, on a human.

Ari sighs before saying, "Napo thinks you need to eat."

I glance back at the raw, slimy seaweed.

"Oh. Um. That's..." I'm about to refuse the snack, when I see Kane's head shaking from the corner of my eye.

All right, then.

"That's very kind. Thank you—Wait." Realization dawns on me. "This is Napo?"

Kane and Ari shoot each other curious looks, nodding their heads as the octopus reaches out, wrapping a tentacle around my wrist before forcing the plant into my hand.

I'm not sure why I expected anything else. After learning that I can breathe underwater and speak with my mind, why wouldn't I have an octopus try to feed me?

The creature gestures between the seaweed and my mouth as if to demonstrate how to eat, and I finally relent. With a brave face, I take a bite. I immediately regret it, but chew and swallow anyway.

Napo pats my arm in a slightly condescending, maternal sort of way while Kane shuffles impatiently. The octopus gives him another pointed look before side-swimming irritably toward the front of the cave, waving for us to follow.

Ari swims up next to me, wrapping an arm around my waist before leading us out of the cave.

A bittersweet feeling takes over me as we glide through the water. Part of me can't help feeling like I might finally be headed toward the answers I've been denied my entire life.

Another part of me wonders if I will survive long enough to get them.

CHAPTER NINE

MELODI

*S*taying alive down here might be easier said than done, at this rate.

Everywhere I turn, something is ready and waiting to kill me.

Or at least that's what Ari keeps insisting.

Everything from the bright corals—or rather, the fish that are hidden among them, some squid that look as if they're wearing striped pajamas, small spotted snails and even the tiniest, most adorable glowing baby jellyfish. It's all dangerous, to me, at least, fragile almost human that I am.

I suppose it shouldn't be surprising considering the home I was raised in. Mother surrounded herself and our chateau with beautiful, deadly things. *Sands*, she raised my sisters to be just that as well.

Still, I can't help but stare in wonder at the world that unfolds around me. Vast orchards of sea-fruits and vegetable farms line the seafloor. There are dense forests of plant life as tall as the palm trees back home and gardens with glowing flowers and sea grass.

I never could have imagined what it would be like to live in the water, what life lurked just beneath the surface of the waves. How many amazing things there were to discover.

Of course, as the time passes, a bit of the wonder does, too, crushed by the weight of my mounting fatigue.

We swim for what feels like days, though the men assure me that it has been far less than even a single hour. The soreness in my muscles says otherwise, but my suggestion that time flows differently beneath the water is quickly shot down.

My temples are throbbing, my aching head and body trying to keep up with the instruction Ari tries to drill into me. Between swimming lessons and never-ending information on the deadly flora and fauna of the sea, I'm struggling to keep up.

When lights appear in the distance, I stop swimming all together.

At first I think it's another reef, but I quickly realize it's so much more.

Ari spins around as we draw closer.

"There is a village ahead," he says, gesturing behind him. "I would tell you to try to blend in—"

"But that will be impossible." Kane chuckles, though the sound is without humor.

"You need to put on a show of strength," Ari continues. "The people will likely acknowledge you in some form. Don't engage them."

He waits for me to nod at that dubious order, ignoring

the questions he no doubt hears swirling in my mind. Why will they acknowledge me? Would that be true if I were anyone?

"Our people pounce on any perceived weakness," Ari continues. "You need to make at least a show of it, or you will not survive here."

I'm not an idiot. I can surmise that the king would punish him for his failure to keep me alive, but I could swear there's something more in Ari's voice than fear for his own sake when he speaks of my survival like a tenuous thing.

Still it grates at me, the way he expects me to cower at every threat on my life when I spent my childhood in the shadow of fear.

"Something new and different for me, then," I say dryly.

He glowers at me. "This isn't a joke, Kala."

But Kane lets out a light laugh. "You have to admit it's getting fairly tiresome."

Ari's blue-green gaze darts between us and he shakes his head.

"It will be more than tiresome if we don't get her to the palace in one piece," Ari mutters with another shake of his head, leading us forward.

The noise grabs my attention first.

Compared to the empty sea, and more than that, to the empty bedroom I spent most of my childhood, this village is *loud*. Chaotic. Fascinating.

The people are all as varied as the barrier reef surrounding us. Brightly colored hair, eyes, and clothes adorn the Mayima, each of them even more beautiful than the last. Some of them wear the same scaled trousers as Ari and Kane—though the women, I note, do have fitted vests that keep their chests firmly in place. It seems more for practicality than modesty, as they come down in a deep, revealing V.

Kane wasn't lying, though. Most are dressed like me in outfits made of netting, accented with shells that often-times highlight the color of their hair.

My escorts swim protectively at my sides, the three of us making a wide berth down the main roads. It isn't long before I understand what Ari and Kane meant before. Even without them acting as my armed guards, the people take note of me.

Their eyes widen in shock when they catch sight of me. More than shock, though, is the unmistakable tremor of fear.

For me? Or for the men at my side?

As we get closer, more than one person bows. They nod to the men next to me, folding an arm across their chest, their fist on the opposite shoulder. But they bow to me, and they use that…word. Insult? Name? Something else entirely?

Kala.

Over and over again. Soon, the crowd around us grows, more people muttering about *Kala. Kala,* as they strain to get a closer look at me.

I try to fortify my shields, but it's hard to focus when I feel the stares of so many faces, each of them focused on my eyes. I think back to the conversation before we left, Kane commenting that I wouldn't be able to blend in. A suspicion is forming in my mind, one I am utterly unprepared for.

"We should go," Ari says in an undertone.

"It won't make a difference," Kane responds in the same volume. "We knew word would spread, and we couldn't very well make the whole trip away from the main currents."

"Still—" But whatever Ari is going to say is cut off by the abrupt sound of deep, booming laughter, followed by a pained cry.

I notice the shadows first, the sharks looming above a cloud of red. They haven't attacked yet. Perhaps they won't, when Kane says that the Mayima have no natural predators. Except for the dragons, of course.

But I am not Mayiman—not entirely—and I have watched sharks just like these devour Mother's victims greedily after she tosses their bloodsoaked bodies into the sea. Fear twists in my gut as the sleek gray shapes glide through the water with an unmistakable air of excitement, waiting and watching the scene unfold below them.

My gaze reluctantly travels there next.

A massive man in scaled armor holds a boy by his neck, his grip tightening as his grin widens. Rivulets of crimson stream out around them, and the boy's arms and legs float at odd angles.

On closer inspection, he must be nearly my age. The fear in his eyes just makes him seem so much younger. My stomach churns, but I keep my features neutral, even as Ari edges in closer, subtly placing his body between mine and the soldier.

"Commander Ariihau," the man greets, hitting his

chest with his fist. It's similar to the gesture the crowd gave us earlier, though more aggressive. "I didn't realize you were here. The honor, of course, is yours."

I don't have time to react to the sound of Ari's full name before the warrior swims closer, extending his victim to Ari like a prize to be had. The nearer they draw, the more my stomach curdles. The smell of blood weighs heavy in my senses, and close up, I can see the shards of bone that jut out from the boy's pallid skin.

The sharks follow like ravenous strays, their shadows swimming back and forth over our heads.

"There is no debt, Sergeant Nikau," Ari says smoothly with a wave of his hand. "The prize is yours."

Prize?

"What is the crime?" Kane asks casually, swimming around the two Mayima, drawing Nikau's attention away from us. I don't miss the careful way he avoids the boy's eyes.

The warrior—Nikau grins widely, his attention turning back toward his victim. His fingers press further into his skin, causing a fresh river of blood to stream out from the wound on his neck.

"Sergeant Kane," he greets with a nod. "Laki, here, is suspected of liaising with the rebels."

The boy shakes his head as much as he can.

"No." His words are loud, and it's an effort not to flinch. "I didn't know who they were—"

He doesn't get a chance to finish the thought before Nikau breaks his neck in one swift motion, not even bothering to go for the silver trident on his back.

It's only once he tosses the body away that the sharks

descend. More like trained hounds than strays, then. Their massive bodies swim past us so fast that the current they leave in their wake nearly knocks me into a somersault.

That movement is what finally draws Nikau's attention to my presence. His mouth drops open, the word *Kala* forming in his mind like a question, before he dips into a bow so deep, I wonder if *he* will spin into a somersault.

"As you see, we have an important mission to tend to," Ari says stiffly. "Tides guide you."

Nikau nods, his wide, tangerine eyes still fixed on me as the Commander leads me away.

We swim silently for miles, all of us locked away in the privacy of our guarded thoughts. When we're far enough away from the village, I finally find myself asking one of the hundreds of questions that are tangling in my mind.

"It's not a name, is it? Kala?"

Ari's face morphs into a thundercloud. He falters for a half second, his arm tensing where it's wrapped around my waist.

"No, Kala," he responds. "It isn't."

Then we are moving again, and the silence descends once more.

CHAPTER TEN

MELODI

There is no more conversation, no more jokes or swimming lessons, only a desperation to get to the next village. Or rather, a ship graveyard.

Instead of colorful, glowing buildings made from giant coral and shells, this place was created from debris and wreckage from my world.

I don't think about how many people died on these ships, or what happened to their bodies. I don't think at all. I keep my mind shut off as we swim toward one of the repurposed ships. It is cracked in half, the masthead pointing upward and a door has been built into the side.

Ari goes ahead, securing one room from the innkeeper. When he's done, he leads us up to the third story to our room.

As haunting as the building appeared on the outside, the room itself feels new, rebuilt from wood that is neither malformed nor decaying.

The men talk quietly in the corner while I take in the space, eager to rid my mind of the graphic images from earlier. To focus on literally anything else besides the hopeless, empty eyes of a dying boy who reminded me far too much of my sister.

Rose was soft, too. And she, too, was murdered at the whim of a monster, though I suspect Mother's motives were more about control than senseless violence. Not that the two are mutually exclusive, not for her, not for anyone.

I take a deep breath, finding that inhaling the sea water serves to be just as calming as inhaling air on land. In, then out, focusing on the things I can see.

Polished sandstone floors and gleaming furniture line the room. Open windows have been carved into the hull, offering a stunning view of mountains and underwater volcanoes in the distance.

A giant pearlescent clamshell rests against the main wall filled with pillows and thin blankets. It's surrounded by long pieces of seaweed—like drapes or curtains and reminds me of the mosquito netting we use on the island.

As soon as I sit down on the sea-sponge mattress, every ounce of exhaustion comes crashing in at once. How long has it been since I slept? Or ate? Or had anything to drink?

How do people hydrate down here? My stomach rumbles, and Napo appears with more seaweed—red this time. I smile down at him, taking the proffered snack. He pats my head approvingly.

I'm already bracing myself for how disgusting it will be, but I take a bite anyway. There aren't a lot of other choices at the moment. Much to my surprise, and relief, it isn't nearly as bad as before. I take another bite and a sweet, peppery flavor glides over my tongue.

It warms me from the inside out. With just two bites, my hunger abates and my thirst is satiated.

"You need to go." Ari's words are louder now, pulling my attention back to the warriors.

His expression is resigned, his arms folded across his chest in a closed off stance as he addresses his cousin. Both of their moods have been markedly worse since the incident earlier.

All three of ours, actually.

My fingers begin moving of their own accord, twisting and braiding and knotting the remaining seaweed in my hands. Napo slides up next to me, bubbles floating from the many movements of his tentacles. He is eyeing me curiously, but not necessarily disdainfully, so I take it as a sign that I can continue.

"So Kala there can poison you in your sleep?" Kane attempts to smile, but it doesn't meet his eyes.

Though his tone is joking, it's clear that he genuinely mistrusts me. And perhaps it's a fair point. If I were either of my sisters, I probably would have already devised a plan to both escape and kill my captors.

Fortunately, that last thought is protected behind my mental shields. Hopefully.

"You know she can't," Ari responds quietly.

Kane runs a hand through his pale pink locks. "No matter…who she is, she is still a danger to you."

Who I am?

It's not the first time they've referenced whatever level of importance I hold, then there were the people in the village. Though I fail to see how that would stop me from harming Ari.

If I'm such an important prisoner, though, why do I only have two guards? Two men against a sea of unrest doesn't seem like such a wise choice. Then again, what do I really know of the politics here? Still, questions race through my mind as my fingers weave the seaweed into a familiar pattern.

"I can handle myself," Ari says with no small amount of exasperation.

"I'm not worried about you handling yourself," Kane bites back, not bothering to keep his voice down. "I'm worried about you handling *her*. Just remember what's at stake here."

"As though I could forget." Ari's tone is dark, and he raises a hand to cut off whatever other objection his cousin was about to make. "Just go. And for sea's sake, send back some marlin."

Kane sighs, giving me one last suspicious sideways glance. "Aye aye, Commander."

He gives Ari what appears to be a slightly mocking salute before turning to go.

I stuff down my questions, knowing the likelihood of getting them answered and frankly, too tired to get into any of it tonight. Tired, and a bit defeated, seeing first-hand that the world I've been thrust into is every bit as violent as the one I hailed from.

Sands, if this is where my mother came from, perhaps that's why she is the way that she is. Perhaps she's one of the kinder Mayima. That's a terrifying thought, but looking at the man who occupies far too much space in this small inn room, I also know it isn't true.

Ari is examining me in turn, inspecting the half-formed creation in my hands.

Or is it Ariihau? Commander Ariihau?

"Commander or Commander Ariihau if there are others around, but...if you slip up, it shouldn't be an issue. They will know you spent this time with Kane."

They? The king and the rest of the court? The other warriors?

I find I'm too drained to ask, so I nod mutely, continuing to work with my fingers moving on reflex.

How many times have I woven a memorial? Too many to count.

It was one tiny way to remember those slain by Mother's hand or by her orders, a way to show that they existed, and that they mattered. One small rebellious act on my part.

Perhaps they had lovers or families to mourn their presence. Someone to miss them and hope for a return that would never come. Maybe, some never had either. And that was all the more reason to create a memorial to show that they weren't wiped away completely.

"What is that?" Ari asks.

"A memorial," I answer him. "For the boy."

He stills in the middle of the room, his arms uncrossing, as he studies me. I don't look up, though. Instead I focus on finishing this project.

"Not your first one," he surmises.

It's not quite a question, but I answer anyway. "No."

Something shifts between us and I wonder if he is

starting to put it together—the life I grew up with. I retreat into my mind, silently accepting another piece of seaweed from Napo to add to the increasingly complicated flower I am creating.

In just a few days, Ari will bring me to the king. I should be wondering more about that, about why the king is looking for me and what he'll do when he has me.

Instead, everything seems to come back to Ari.

Why did I see his face every night for weeks? Why does the world feel quieter when he's around?

They're questions I suspect he knows the answer to, since every time I catch his gaze it's already on me. I take stock of my mental shields again, making sure they're firmly in place and that he can't hear my thoughts.

A small twitch of his lips tells me he notices, but he doesn't say anything. Silently, he disappears into a small room off to the side, one I can only assume is a bathing chamber.

When I finish with the memorial, I hang it in the window, unsure what to do with it. Only then do I fully realize the situation as it stands. I'm exhausted, and ready for sleep. After the day we've had, I'm sure Ari is, too.

But there is only one bed.

CHAPTER ELEVEN

MELODI

*A*ri returns from the lavatory, his skin smooth and clean. I want to freshen up before bed too, but I'm not even sure where to begin.

He nods, and gestures toward the small room. Of course, my thought was louder than I meant it to be. It's even harder to moderate them when I'm this tired.

Still, I'm grateful because I would have had no idea of what to do in here.

Pointing to a small bowl of white sand, he explains that this is used to clean your skin. There are flowers growing along the wall, and their oils can be obtained by crushing the leaves. Those are for your hair.

And finally, a short bench in the corner that is somehow attached to pipes that lead to a sinkhole will dispose of the necessary bodily functions.

Once I feel like I understand everything, I shoo Ari from the room, shutting the door behind him.

I take my time, rubbing handfuls of sand along my

skin, scrubbing away the debris from the day. The flowers smell like peonies and soon my hair does too. I try to collect my thoughts as I clean up. But my mind keeps drifting back to one thing.

One bed.

It shouldn't matter. After the day I've had, the blood-shed we've seen, I shouldn't care. It would almost be easier if the thought of our shared sleeping arrangement were as distressing as it should be. But my traitorous body doesn't seem to care that we don't know a single thing about this gorgeous, guarded man.

In fact, my skin is practically vibrating with excitement at the idea of being closer to him. Of lying next to him on the bed, and closer than that.

Ari rubs a hand over his face, squeezing his eyes shut and looking like he is praying to whatever Mayiman deity he believes in.

I must have let my shields drop again.

"We're sharing the bed?" I ask somewhat unnecessarily.

"It's not sexual for Mayima when we share a bed. It's practicality. Kane and I would have done the same." With Ari's overly neutral tone and the way his gaze rakes over me, I wonder if he's giving the explanation for my benefit as much as he's reminding himself.

"Of course," I say with equal nonchalance.

He narrows his eyes like he suspects that I am biting back laughter at his expense. Which is fair, because I definitely am. He turns away, stretching while he pretends to ignore me. The muscles in his back ripple with the movement, and I don't have the energy to pretend to ignore him in turn.

Sighing for the hundredth time today, he unbuckles the strap that holds his trident, placing it on the ground next to him before gracefully climbing into the bed. Napo slides onto the other side of the mattress. He takes a few moments to plump the pillows before he lays his head down, and I swear there's something mischievous in his squishy features at leaving me the space in the middle.

Right next to Ari.

The glance Ari gives the octopus confirms my thoughts. With a sigh that mirrors my captor's, I lie down in the narrow space, trying to ignore how I feel instantly calmer with the proximity.

After a few tense moments, I risk glancing over at him.

For all that he says sharing a bed isn't sexual here, I struggle to feel the truth of that when he's next to me, shirtless, heat radiating from him and sending tendrils of fire dancing along my skin. His sure, strong hands clench, and I can't help but picture them sliding along my shoulders, down to my waist, his throaty growl sounding in my head, his...

"You need to stop, Kala." Each word is truncated.

A flush burns through me. I should apologize, but instead, I find myself asking the obvious question. "Why?"

"Because it's dangerous." He doesn't seem to want to say this.

"Dangerous for who?"

"For both of us," he grudgingly admits.

Is that better? Worse? He has all but admitted this is not one sided in the same breath as he completely dismisses it. Something like grief washes over me, more potent than it has a right to be in the circumstances.

"Why?" I ask again, the word more frustrated this time.

I have been here less than a day, and already, I am sick of the way I understand nothing about this place.

"There are things I can't tell you." He seems to be responding to my quieter thought as much as the one I intentionally projected, though my mental shields feel secure.

"Then tell me something." It's more of a plea than a demand, and perhaps that's why he doesn't say no out of hand.

Perhaps he can sense the way the day is finally edging in on me, fraying at the fabric of my sanity. The way the strange thrumming between us is driving me mad with wanting and confusion.

The fact that watching someone die never gets any easier.

Ari gives a curt nod.

"There are three classes of Mayima," he begins, the deep, calm timbre of his voice instantly soothing me. "Nobility, Warriors, and Traders, or the villagers. Your class is decided by birth, and it cannot change."

"And you were born a Warrior." It's not really a question.

He told me his clothes belonged to a warrior, and he goes by Commander. It explains why he serves such a cruel master, when he is not an inherently cruel person. Like my sisters, he has no choice.

"I was," he confirms. His tone is hesitant, like he's

waiting for my judgment, so I let my shields drop enough for him to see that there is none.

He relaxes incrementally, offering me further explanation. "That's what the tattoos mean."

Do I imagine the smug tilt to his lips? He certainly knows I have noticed his tattoos. Several, several times. That thought leaks out, and though he has said these feelings are dangerous, satisfaction rolls off of him in waves.

"They're lines for each challenge I've won."

I think of the respect offered to him today, the fear. "Is that how you climb ranks? Or are you born into that, too?"

"Not born into it. We can challenge anyone to claim their rank." He doesn't have to tell me that Commander is one of the higher ranks, based on what I witnessed earlier.

"What constitutes a win?"

He levels me with a look, and I realize how naive the question was after what I've witnessed today. They fight to the death. Of course they do.

"Does that bother you?" he asks, carefully guarding the rest of his mind so I can't get even a hint of what he's feeling.

I ponder the question. Perhaps it should, but it feels high-handed to judge a culture I know nothing about. What bothers me the most is realizing that Ari's rank is likely sought after. That anyone can challenge him at any time.

"I can take care of myself, Kala." His tone is warmer than it has been, and I wonder if his fatigue is getting to him the way mine is getting to me.

"Thank you for telling me that," I say instead of responding. "And for keeping me safe today."

His features close off at that, and he all but scoffs. I get the feeling the bitterness is directed at himself more than it is at me.

"Don't thank me yet, Kala."

CHAPTER TWELVE

REMY

*E*inar finds me at the quarterdeck.

He must have taken his tonic, because his legs are far less shaky now than they were earlier. Wordlessly, I hand him the bottle of whiskey that has been keeping me company this evening.

I know it weighs on everyone, the fact that I'm keeping more and more to myself and running through our booze supply with abandon.

But I don't relish talking much these days. And likely won't until I can bring my sisters the vengeance we deserve. Stars, the vengeance we all deserve, the man at my side included.

Madame has haunted us all for far too long.

Einar takes a long sip from the bottle before passing it back. He doesn't say anything, just stares at the night sky, like me. His presence is calming, steady, not unlike my father's. He looks young, not too much older than me, and sometimes it's easy to forget that they were friends for longer than I have been alive.

The thought brings a pang that I've been trying to escape. I take another swig of whiskey, hoping to bury the feeling in the haze of alcohol.

I don't want to think about either of my parents.

"It will get easier," Einar says after a long bout of silence.

I squeeze my eyes shut and take another dreg from the bottle. I'm not sure if he's talking about his grief for my parents, or for the family he lost when he was even younger than me, but right now, I'm not sure it matters.

I can't imagine a world where this pain doesn't last, where I forget them long enough to move on.

"You mean when we get our vengeance?"

He gives me a long, measuring look. "Is that why you're here?"

I raise my eyebrows. "Isn't that why we're all here?"

"No. I wouldn't risk any of this just to get back at her, no matter what she's done. I'm here for the life I can have on the other side of it." Einar glances significantly toward where Zaina is still in their cabin. "The one that's only possible when Ulla is dead."

Swallowing hard, I pass him the bottle once again.

"I'm not ready to think about that yet," I admit.

It feels wrong, the idea of moving on with my day-to-day life when my brother is dead and my parents are dead.

Einar sighs, taking a drink. "No one ever is."

WHEN I SLIP BACK into the cabin I share with Aika, she is in the middle of undressing.

Her fingers deftly work the top laces on her corset with a practiced ease, her dark eyes scanning me over her shoulder. For a moment, I'm transported to a different room, where I am the one undoing the laces, slowly stripping her bare and relishing each inch of skin as it's unveiled before me.

I shake the thought away, leaning casually against the closed door.

"Funny how you don't seem to need help with your corset now," I say with all of the nonchalance I don't feel.

Her hands pause in their work. It's impossible to sneak up on her, so I know I haven't surprised her, but perhaps my teasing tone has. Slowly, she turns to face me, her light skirts swaying with the movement. The moonlight catches on her ivory skin, highlighting her gentle curves and toned muscles. Her eyes meet mine, mischief mingling with something else. Something more vulnerable, almost like hope.

It hurts, like everything does these days. Still, I don't look away, and neither does she.

"I could have sworn you had seen me undoing my corset before," she says, arching an obsidian eyebrow before undoing her long braid. Her raven hair falls sleekly over her shoulders, concealing her body more than I care for.

"It must have slipped my mind." The words come out devoid of the warmth I meant to inject in them.

"Right," she says quietly, her voice less playful than before.

She turns back around then, trying to hide the defeat in the slump of her shoulders. Before I even register the steps it takes to get to her, I'm closing the gap between us, wrapping my arms around her and pulling her back against me.

"Or maybe I just wanted to touch you," I say softly, emphasizing my words by running my fingers along the curve of her hips.

A small gasp escapes her, and she arches back into me.

"Maybe I just wanted you to touch me," she whispers.

Sliding her hair over one shoulder, I place my lips on her neck, kissing her wildly thrumming pulse.

"I've missed you," she breathes, leaning further into my touch.

"I know."

There is nothing else to say. I know I've been absent. I know she's been trying. I know that it took everything she had to break down her walls and let me on the other side, and how much it must have hurt her when I shut her out.

It's easier to show her that I'm sorry than to say it, so I graze my teeth along her skin, biting down gently until she lets out a gasp.

Words have never been our strong suit. We use them more often to spar than communicate, but this—this is a language we speak fluently.

She brings her arms up, reaching behind her to fist her hands in my hair. A growl escapes me and I abandon her half-laced corset, moving to untie her skirt instead. It falls to the floor, leaving her in only her lacy undergarments.

And her corset, of course.

She spins in my arms, propping herself back on the

bolted down dresser and pulling me with her. I sink to my knees before her, kissing my way from her ankle to her thigh on first one leg, then the other. Greedily, I soak in the sight of her, then the taste, as I trail my lips along her skin.

She said she missed me, but I've missed her, too. I've missed being close to her in this way, in every way, missed the way that she reacts to my touch in perfect synchrony like we are tethered together by our very beings.

I have missed everything about her, and I take the time to slowly, methodically show her just that.

I may not be ready to move past the grief, or as willing to let go of my need for vengeance as Einar seems to be, but I won't waste any more time hiding from my wife.

Not when our time feels perilously short as it is.

CHAPTER THIRTEEN

MELODI

The night was restless, filled with vivid dreams of the warrior who slept at my side.

More than once, I thought I dreamt his solid arms around me only to wake up shivering with a solid foot of space between us, Napo's enormous purple and teal tentacles curling on the pillow by my face.

Ari doesn't look any more rested than I feel. He slowly blinks as he separates the netting and climbs from the bed, making his way to the lavatory with bloodshot eyes. The sound of the door latching shut echoes in a warbled way.

Napo throws the coverlet to the bottom of the bed, rising to stretch out his long tentacles. His black eyes meet mine, and he seems to smile at me. Ambling forward, he pulls back the netting, clambering out to the open space, and reaches for one of the small fish swimming around the room.

He grabs ahold of it, and then unfurls his limb to offer it to me. Presumably, to eat.

No.

My stomach growls, but not for that very much alive, very much struggling fish. Just like he did with the seaweed, Napo stretches a tentacle forward insistently, placing the squirming fish in my hands.

It looks at me with pleading eyes as it fights to get back to freedom. Am I supposed to eat it like this? To put it out of its misery first? Napo looks pleased, giving me some version of a nod in response. Bubbles froth from the fish's mouth as its eyes lock onto mine in silent horror.

My eyes track the slow movement of the smaller group of fish that have been entering through the open window. A few of them swim headfirst into the wall before rerouting. They don't seem nearly as intelligent as the fish held between my hands.

Why couldn't I have ended up with one of those?

The question doesn't matter. I have no intention of tasting anything as it watches me doing so.

I think of the innuendo my middle sister would make out of that, picturing Ari's face and the ridges of his muscles as a reluctant smile tugs at my lips. The bathing chamber door is wrenched open so suddenly that a flurry of bubbles accompany Ari as he exits, a thunderous expression on his perfect features.

"Kala, you—" He freezes when he catches sight of me, his rebuke abruptly cutting off.

I follow his gaze to find that my netted top is askew, putting on display the few parts of me that were adequately covered yesterday. His jaw clenches, and he pointedly averts his gaze to the ceiling.

Releasing the fish, I quickly cover myself. I can't bring

myself to be sorry to see the fish go. I would rather be hungry than eat a living, slimy thing. Napo gives me a disapproving glare at the loss of breakfast, but stretches out a few tentacles to help me adjust my top anyway.

"We'll order food," Ari says, shooing the fish out the open window on his way back to the bathing chamber while Napo eyes him disdainfully. "In the meantime, practice your shields."

He sends that last part like a warning. An order he has every expectation of being followed. I consider his explanation last night, the way the one thing he chose to explain to me was the class systems. If you're born into a class and you don't leave it, it stands to reason you don't marry outside of it.

Is that why my attraction to him is dangerous?

Does that mean I am from a different class? Or is it because I am half human? I think again about *Kala*, the bowing, hardly wanting to piece together the obvious.

I'm sure I'll find out soon enough.

True to his word, Ari orders breakfast, and I'm pleased to see it's more than just seaweed. Though there is, of course, seaweed.

But there's also a platter of raw fish, with slices of different fruits and grains. We eat with our hands, using the seaweed to scoop up each bite.

It's delicious. And most importantly, it doesn't stare at me with wide, judgmental eyes.

The corner of Ari's mouth tilts up, and I could swear I get a hint of amusement from him. I glance over at him from the corner of my eye.

"Something funny?" I ask.

"No," he lies.

"Really?" I press. "Because I could have sworn I saw you smirk."

"You must not be able to see well through the water with your human eyes."

"Well I can hear your chuckle just fine with my Mayiman mind," I say wryly.

He shakes his head, his stern expression firmly back in place and his walls feeling even more solid than they had a moment ago. My shoulders sag a little, in spite of myself. I miss my sisters, Aika's bawdy sense of humor and Zaina's quieter one.

Ari lets out what appears to be his underwater version of a sigh. "Napo...he's always had interesting ways with food."

"Oh?"

"Octopii are the only thing in our kingdom not strictly controlled by the king," he explains. "But Napo is one of the few I've seen who deliberately takes advantage of that. He has force fed many a warrior those tiny, live fish, and food off the king's plate."

A soundless laugh escapes me.

"Has he always been your pet?" I ask.

Ari shakes his head in warning, but it's too late. Something connects with my leg—the tiny biting fish Napo has lobbed at me.

"Not your pet, then?"

"No," he says, holding back what I am fairly certain is a laugh. "Just a willing companion. We don't have pets here."

"My apologies, Napo," I say.

He folds two of his tentacles.

"Sincerely," I add. "There is no excuse for my ignorance. Please...forgive me."

Reluctantly, he nods. Then he offers me another live fish, his eyes daring me not to take it. Ignoring Ari's barely suppressed amusement, I take the fish.

I bite its little head off, chewing it up and swallowing it before the scent can waft up to me on a salty wave of sea air.

And I smile at Napo the whole time.

AFTER BREAKFAST, we head outside, and I brace myself for another long day of swimming. As it turns out, I needn't have bothered.

A pair of large, elongated black fish wait outside. They each have armored saddles with a high-backed seat. Sharp metal covers their long, spear shaped noses, turning them into swords.

Send back some marlins, Ari had told Kane. This was nothing at all what I had expected.

"Climb up," Ari instructs.

The marlin is staring ahead, not paying me any attention. It looks tame enough, but there are no bridles, nothing to hold onto. I've never so much as ridden a horse.

With all of the enthusiasm of someone forced to handle a fetid, rotting corpse, Ari reaches out and places a hand on either side of my waist, lifting me up and positioning me on the saddle. He guides my leg into the open strap on the side, buckling it solidly around my thigh.

His skin is warm on mine, igniting me everywhere he touches. I bite down on my lip, picturing solid brick walls, the steel of Aika's swords, the iron gates around Mother's estate, literally anything to serve as a barrier between his mind and mine.

His grimace tells me he knows what thoughts I'm shutting him out from, but his lack of chastisement tells me I'm succeeding. He repeats the process with my other leg, his touch just as perfunctory and removed.

Which is for the best.

Only when I am completely secure does he raise his eyes to meet mine.

"The marlins are intuitive, and yours will follow the lead of mine."

I nod my affirmation, taking a moment to greet my fish while he mounts his. Napo swims up to settle in behind Ari, wrapping his tentacles around his shoulders and settling his body on top of the high-backed seat. If the massive man is unhappy about this arrangement, he at least hides it moderately well.

Not that I can blame him, having experienced Napo's displeasure for myself. I think it's more than that, though. Ari clearly has a soft spot for the octopus.

Before I can think too hard about it, we're taking off at a lightning speed. My fish tilts side to side with the currents, spinning at wild angles and dipping rapidly with the changing waters. Now I understand the need for the straps, and the backing.

However Ari is directing his marlin, mine does,

indeed, follow just behind, diving and darting through the water in perfect sync with its companion. The ocean passes by in a blur, an array of colors and lights and sea creatures we are moving far too fast for my eyes to linger on. The water whips through my hair, stinging my eyes if I keep them open for too long.

As it is, I have just enough time to duck out of the way of small fish or debris. I'm not complaining, though. It's a convenient distraction from the torrent of questions that won't let me rest.

From wondering how long the ghost of Ari's fingertips will haunt me this time.

CHAPTER FOURTEEN

MELODI

$\mathcal{T}$ime is difficult to gauge down here.

The sunlight filters through the layers of waves into a wan imitation of itself, and the glow from the sea creatures is hardly consistent. Between the hours we've been riding and the darkness falling around us, I hazard a guess that it's close to sundown when a new sound hits my ears—my real ears, not just the part of my brain that has become accustomed to mind-speak.

It's almost like...music. Enchanting and strange, unlike anything I've ever heard before, but melodic all the same.

"What is that?" I ask Ari, my neck craning in the direction of the sound.

He eyes me cautiously before answering. "The villagers are dancing."

Dancing. A memory hits me.

I ask Zaina to play, hoping we can infuse the smallest bit of life into a day that has done nothing but rob us of it.

Hoping that if she remembers Rose, it might help to soften the jagged shards of ice that are slowly taking over her soul.

So she sits at the piano, her perfect face nearly as devoid of life as Mother's victims were today. Aika stands behind her, taking her cue from our oldest sister even though she would never admit it. She throws herself into the song, playing her violin so violently, I think the bow might break.

And I lose myself in the music they create, trying to ignore the sinking feeling that permeates the air.

I have already lost one sister. How long until I lose the others? Aika is reckless and Zaina is drowning. One way or another, it seems that Mother will take them both from me.

But at least she's gone tonight.

So, I swallow the pain building inside of me, throwing every part of myself into the dance. I ignore the memories of bloodshed. The threat that lingers over us like a constant shadow.

I pretend we're on a different balcony, in a different tower, in a different world, far from the hold that Mother has on us all. Where we aren't prisoners. Where we are free.

It is the only small rebellion I ever allow myself, this bit of happiness, of peace, when I know that Mother approves of neither.

I only wish I could grant some semblance of it to my sisters.

My chest aches at the memory and with the weight of missing them, but there's something else there, too. Desire to feel that freedom again. How do the Mayima dance? Do they lose themselves the way that I do?

"Can we go?" I ask.

"It's dangerous," he responds, the words coming to his lips automatically.

"Everything is dangerous," I counter.

Everything here. Everything on land. Everything with *him*. That's no reason not to take a rare reprieve where we can find one, but I suspect that's not a mindset Ari would agree with.

Sure enough, he doesn't respond.

Earlier, he said that the marlins are intuitive, and I have spent my entire day showering mine with attention. I try to direct some of my will at it, coaxing it with my thighs, and am rewarded when it goes in the direction of the song.

Ari's curse sounds in my head, but he doesn't immediately stop me, though I have no doubt that he could.

We draw closer until I take in what might be the most magical sight I've ever beheld. Glowing coral lines the sand, and colorful jellyfish float around the air, lighting up the dim space. Schools of tiny, bright fish weave through the crowd of Mayima.

But it's the dancing that catches my eye. They move like the music is a part of them, like it's resonating in their bodies and souls, melding into their very being. It's graceful and artistic and almost haunting.

I may not be able to swim like they do, but this...this I can do.

"Kala." Ari's warning sounds behind me. "You've seen. Now, let's go."

He says this with all of the authority of a man who is used to his every order being obeyed. A Commander. But I have grown up in Madame's household.

Orders are nothing new for me. Neither is danger. And this, dancing, is the closest thing I've ever had to something that's mine, the one thing she could never take from me, the thing that brought me closer to my sisters.

For all that I have been compliant, I am not an idiot.

The king might kill me when I arrive. He might do worse. This might be the last chance I have to enjoy anything ever again.

So I meet Ari's eyes, letting him see the rare bit of defiance in mine.

"You lured me here," I say quietly.

If he is surprised I put that together from his conversation with Kane, Ari doesn't show it.

"You lured me into the water with your song, where your cousin kidnapped me, and I have done everything you asked without complaint even when we both know you're keeping secrets." I unbuckle the holster at my left thigh. "Even when we both know that my obedience might be leading me straight to my death."

Without breaking eye contact, I unbuckle the holster on the right. He doesn't move to stop me.

"Is this one dance really so much to ask?" I push.

His features tighten into an unreadable mask as he unbuckles his own holster. I slide off my marlin, stretching my legs. I am sore, but my body isn't as heavy in the water. It's nothing I can't manage.

"One dance," he finally responds, the words searing into my head. "I will stand guard."

I can't help the small smile that breaks across my face as I head into the throng of Mayima. It isn't hard to emulate their movements, the seductive thrusts of their hips and lilt of their arms that feel almost primal in nature. It isn't long before I lose myself in the beat, the energy, the pulse of music that reverberates down into my soul.

A voice pulls me from my thoughts.

"You look like you could use a partner."

It's too dark for me to make out the features, but the tone is kind, appreciative. The glow around us highlights the tilt of a masculine chin as the Mayima scans my body from head to toe.

Though his isn't the attention I want, I can't deny a small bit of satisfaction, being viewed as something desirable in a simple, innocuous way. Not a deity to be revered or an ornament to be protected. Just a woman in a crowd in need of a dance partner.

Before I can respond, a deep growl startles us both. Well, it startles the man asking me to dance. Some part of me has been half-expecting it since the man spoke up.

Wanting it.

Needing it.

"She already has a partner." There is no mistaking the authority in Ari's tone.

Do I have a partner?

Ari looks at me as though he hears my response, despite my shields. Perhaps he is only learning to read me the way I am him.

"Co-commander," the man stutters a bit before recovering himself. "Apologies, I was unaware. The debt is mine."

"Return to your home, and there will be no debt."

How very magnanimous of him. I resist the urge to arch an eyebrow, wondering if I am imagining the hint of amusement that emanates from his mind to mine.

"Sir." He swims away faster than I can track, and I turn my full attention to Ari.

"Was that necessary?" I ask him, my body still swaying with the music.

"Yes." Like he can't stop himself, he closes the distance between us, putting his hands on my waist.

His thumbs graze my exposed hipbones, and I lean into his touch.

It doesn't surprise me to see him moving in perfect timing with the beat. To feel him guiding my body in synchrony with his. I turn in his arms, putting my back to him as I see many of the Mayima around me doing.

I can't deny that I have wanted this from the moment I saw the dancers on the floor. His hands on my body. His warmth against mine.

"Kala." He growls the word like a warning, but I don't bother to be embarrassed this time, not when he pulls me tighter against him.

He has one hand trailing my arm while the other is flush against my ribcage, drumming out a tantalizing beat in time with the song. My heart thunders wildly in my chest, but it's not the only one. I can hear his, too, feel it echoing in my soul, the perfect complement to mine.

Some deeply carnal part of me hums in satisfaction at his closeness as he sweeps my hair to one side, burying his face in my neck.

One dance, he had said. But when the song changes, he doesn't move. And a thousand black marlin couldn't pull me from this spot.

Two dances turn into three, then five, until I am facing him once more. His features are obscured, but it still feels like I am drowning in his sea green gaze. The echo of it. The memory of it.

Then the music cuts off at the end of the final song. The spell is broken.

Ari's hands disappear from my body, and every part of me mourns the loss. I know what he is going to say even before his voice sounds in my head.

"We can't do that again."

I want to ask him why, but I know he won't give me the answer, certainly not now when he looks like he's barely restraining himself from touching me again.

So instead I give him the easy acquiescence I've become accustomed to, avoiding what we both already know.

"I know." I want to mean it, but my heart is still pounding, my skin still zapping from its contact with his.

If he senses that I'm lying, he doesn't bother to call me out. He only slams his shields down tighter as he gestures for us to leave, shutting me out of his mind.

As usual.

CHAPTER FIFTEEN

MELODI

*T*hat night, when we fall into bed, it's with the full weight of the dance between us.

And Napo.

Ari is quick to position the octopus between us, along with a mountain of pillows. He turns to face the wall as Napo curls into my side. The octopus stretches out his tentacles, wrapping them around me protectively. Within moments, his inky eyes are drifting closed and he's drifting off to sleep.

Which makes one of us.

Ari is too still for someone who is actually sleeping, and I seem to be having the opposite problem. There's a restlessness in my limbs that won't abate.

"Peace, Kala," Ari says, his neutral tone edged with weariness.

I'm not even sure what's keeping me awake at this point, the residual energy from our dance or the things I forced myself to come to terms with earlier. All my life, I have been surrounded by death, but I have never felt it looming before me the way I'm starting to now.

"You aren't going to die." His words linger in the water around us for several moments before I bring myself to respond.

"How do you know?"

"Because I won't let that happen."

I don't know exactly how this mind-speak works, if the determination I feel from him is real, or merely a projection of what I want to hear, but his words soothe me from the inside out, quelling some of the agitation in my veins. In spite of our situation and the secrets he keeps, I believe him.

When I finally drift off to sleep, though, it's short-lived.

Nightmares chase me off and on for hours, the restless feeling swelling to a crescendo until it wrestles me from sleep time and again. By the time I abandon my attempt entirely, Ari is already up and stretching in the center of the room. Judging by the taut set of his shoulders and his hardened expression, it's clear that he didn't fare much better than I did.

The rest of the day is edged with tension. It thrums between us, twisting and choking and threatening to drive me mad. All throughout breakfast and well into our arduous ride through swift currents, Ari is careful to keep his walls up, but his eyes tighten or his fists clench often enough to tell me I'm not alone in this feeling.

He doesn't allow a single, stray thought to escape, even when one of the many deadly sea creatures makes an appearance. Though he is at my side, pulling me deftly from harm, he says nothing.

The silence is deafening.

Sound travels more slowly down here than at the surface. So though there are whales in the distance and bubbling from sea animals closer by, the steady rush of the current in my ear, it's not the same as the constant swell of the sea that I have spent my life with, both in Delphine and Corentin.

Around what I assume is late afternoon, we stop for a snack—a term I use loosely for the very nutritious and not remotely delicious seaweed Napo insists on plying me with. Even the sound of the water in my ears is gone, then, leaving the kind of silence that soaks into my bones, putting me on edge.

Ari looks over at me, something that might be guilt lurking behind his eyes.

"Kala," he begins, his tone more reserved than usual.

But whatever he is about to say is abruptly cut off. His features turn to ice, his hand unsheathing his trident in a single fluid motion as he turns his attention to something behind me.

There is murder in his eyes, and his muscles strain against his skin as if they're trying to break free. Right now, he looks as if he could battle a dragon itself and come out the victor.

I follow his line of sight, spinning in time to see several warriors approaching in the distance, just before Ari places himself between us. His words feel different when he speaks this time, closer somehow and more intimate, despite the warning they carry.

"Say nothing," he orders, and I nod on instinct. "Prepare the marlin and be ready for a quick escape."

He doesn't wait for a response before darting out to meet the group of warriors, speeding through the water faster than anything I've witnessed so far.

A tentacle slowly wraps around my wrist, tugging me backward and I don't want to go. Logically, I know I can't fight, but my instincts tell me to stay. Napo's instincts, however, are prodding me toward the expectant fish.

He stays next to me, as I climb into the saddle, his tentacles spreading out as if he is my own personal shield. My pulse is racing—violently beating against my chest in anticipation. I'm too far away to hear their words, but I can feel the moment when everything changes, just before the set of Ari's shoulders stiffens.

In one fell swoop, he takes out two of the warriors.

Then red fills the water around them as their lifeless bodies float away, fodder for the sharks who will no doubt be along shortly to claim their prize.

CHAPTER SIXTEEN

MELODI

The world has turned into a hazy blur.

Blood clouds the water, tingeing everything pink. The blur of bodies. The flash of weapons. Napo's tentacle, as he prods me to strap my legs into the harness.

My fingers fumble and slip, distracted as I am by the fray.

The lightning fast movements are impossible to track, but time and again I catch sight of Ari, attacking with expert precision whenever one of the Mayima tries to slip past him. For all that Madame has forced me to bear witness to her savagery in the past, it's me who can't look away now. Not when Ari makes protecting me a thing of art, even in its brutality.

The pink in the water turns to a darker red, and somewhere in the chaos, I lose sight of Ari entirely. Frantically, I search for his blue-green hair, his distinctive gold trident, anything to tell me where he is.

But he is lost among the moving bodies. And the unmoving ones.

Something inside of me flares to life. An unreasonable fury and fear that propels me into action. Instinctively, I slam my barriers into place, locking out any whisper of thought as I cement my plan.

I know that it makes no sense. I tell myself that, even as I will the marlin forward. I'm trapped between instinct and logic, unable to make myself stop, to think this through, to listen to reason even as I take myself through the litany of reasons that I should stay put.

I can't fight. I have never trained. The Mayima are fierce, ruthless. Taking them on is the equivalent to challenging Mother herself.

Still, I prod my marlin toward the fray, pulled by an invisible tether. My panic ebbs incrementally with each bit of distance I cover between me and Ari. Leaning forward in my saddle, I apply pressure to the fish with my calves and heels, just like Ari taught me, urging him to go faster. To head straight into the battle.

I feel, more than see, Napo wrapping his tentacles around my waist, hanging on tightly as we slice through the water at a blinding speed.

Groans of pain and grunts of exertion sound all around me, the crimson in the sea clearing just long enough for more to replace it. I don't even let myself consider that any of it might belong to Ari.

It can't.

Two more bodies float upward. They're both unfamiliar, but I'm not so naive as to be relieved yet.

We circle the fighting men until I finally spot him—the golden glint of his trident and teal hair standing in stark contrast to the other Mayima.

He's incredible to watch. Each arc of his weapon, each blow he lands—it cements the feeling of safety inside of me. Safety, and something else I can't quite name.

As he locks tridents with one Mayima, though, a female warrior goes for his back. I have seen enough of Ari's prowess to know he will probably end this quickly and spin in time.

Probably.

But that irrational, panicked part of me is already propelling me into motion, unwilling to risk the chance that this is the time he falters. Spurring the marlin forward, I aim for the attacking warrior. I have no idea if this will work, and do my best to allow the fish to feel my intentions. He flies through the water, directly toward the fighter with the golden hair. Ari spins and catches sight of me, along with one of the others, but it's too late.

Before anyone can react, we crash into our target, the marlin's armored bill spearing clean through the female warrior. The coppery tang of blood fills my senses as we swim through the hazy red. Am I imagining the way it burns my eyes? The way it fills my nose and coats my throat?

It's an effort not to lose the precious few contents of my stomach as the fish shakes her free. She's badly injured, but not quite dead yet. I glance back over my shoulder just as Ari's mount arrives, the gleaming silver of its armor piercing through the woman once again.

He pushes her back toward Ari, who raises his trident to finish the job.

With one smooth arc of his weapon, the woman's head is no longer attached to her body. My hands shake. My stomach seizes. Ari's voice is in my head, a distant melody that I can't quite focus on but try to tether myself to, all the same.

The marlin turns around, either at his prodding or at mine.

My eyes have barely locked back onto him when I feel a white-hot pain lance through me. It steals my breath, and I double over in shock as my legs grip the saddle. My hand darts to my exposed skin, but where I expect warm blood to pool between my fingers, there is nothing but sea water.

There is no injury. No weapon protruding from my ribs, nothing but the smooth skin that was there before.

It doesn't make any sense. The phantom pain lingers and my mind races. Some weapons are more discreet than others. I do a quick calculation of the things I've eaten, the things I've touched—wondering if I've been poisoned somewhere along the way.

I glance up just as Ari spears the final warrior with his trident. He stops moving, slumping forward as a gush of blood rushes out of him. Ari uses his trident to push the body away. Disgust or fury mar his perfect features as he moves closer. He calls for his marlin, struggling to secure his feet in the stirrups, hand clenching his side.

"Are you hurt?" I ask, momentarily forgetting about my own pain.

He doesn't bother to answer, his teeth grinding together instead.

Movement pulls my attention upward. Sharks have already arrived, circling like vultures, ready and waiting for permission to consume the dead.

"We need to get out of here," Ari says before slamming his walls up once again.

Napo leaves my saddle to join Ari in his. His large, round eyes study the Commander's face in concern, before he wraps himself around Ari's wound, like a living bandage.

Within seconds, we're gone, our fish taking off at a breakneck speed that throws me backward in my saddle. We don't communicate for miles, but my thoughts haunt me nonetheless.

I know it was stupid to dive headfirst into a fight, to be another distraction for Ari. But there was something primal about it that I couldn't resist. I wonder if he understands that. If he always fights the way he did today, or if he is helpless against an irrational need to keep me safe. Alive.

The same way that I am with him.

CHAPTER SEVENTEEN

MELODI

*H*ours pass before we stop for the night—hours where I am consumed by worry for Ari and thoughts of a dying Mayima warrior. A warrior I all but killed.

There was no satisfaction when the life left her eyes. Perhaps that's enough to set me apart from my mother. I can't dredge up any real remorse, either, though. Not when she was going to kill Ari.

Nor can I find moral superiority in standing by while someone kills in defense of me rather than entering the fray to return the favor. Still, I regret the necessity, the senseless violence that seems to permeate every last molecule of space in my life.

Despite my insistence that we break to tend to his wound, Ari pushes us until the waters are as dark as a starless night in the middle of the forest. I can't see my hand in front of my face, let alone the man at my side. But I can sense his pain—his exhaustion. He's struggling more than he normally does to keep his shields in place.

When my marlin slows, I hear voices in the distance. Not long after, I see the gentle glow of a pale blue light. *Another village?* The light grows brighter, revealing a settlement much larger than the other villages we've passed. More like a town. Glowing algae covers the buildings made of coral, the shell-lined streets and the abandoned ships that they've repurposed as shops and inns.

Once again, everyone greets Ari reverentially, calling him by his title, and when their eyes finally meet mine, I'm not surprised by the word that follows. Haunting me like my own shadow—*Kala*.

Even the innkeeper greets us with special attention once we dismount in front of his building. His eyes linger on us for too long, his head bowed in respect while he orders a young boy to tend to our mounts. He ushers us in quickly, showing us to our chamber and informing us that dinner will be brought up before we can even ask.

Ari wastes no time in bolting our door closed, further securing it with his trident. Then, with a groan, he sits down heavily on the bed's edge and winces as he pulls Napo from his injury.

My hand reflexively goes to my side, pain still radiating from somewhere deep under my skin. In the exact same spot as the laceration that Ari is now inspecting.

His gaze flickers up to my hand, and he looks away with a grimace—but not a single trace of surprise. His mental shields harden even more, and the pain I'm feeling disappears. This can't be normal. I certainly didn't feel the injuries of the other Mayima.

"Don't," Ari says before I can form the question in my mind.

He's tired and in pain from an injury he received protecting me today. Though I do want answers, I certainly don't need them before we even treat his wound. So I nod, fixing my attention on the slice along his ribcage.

"What can I do?"

He looks like he wants to argue, but instead, gestures gruffly to the medical kit Napo has produced from our travel pack. The octopus withdraws several long pieces of glowing seaweed, and a few of those long, spiral shells. It takes me a moment to recall the name. *Auger.*

Ari points to one of the shells. "That one first."

I take it, unsure what to do with it.

"There's a stopper," he explains.

Sure enough, I see it once I know what to look for.

Inside is a thick, sap-like mixture he instructs me to spread onto the cut. A hiss of pain lances through me once again, but Ari's features reveal nothing, nor does he comment. Napo hands over a fuzzy plant that looks like algae, and it adheres itself to the wound.

Finally, I unstopper two more auger shells—one white and one pink. These contain brightly colored beads that he pours into his mouth. All the while, Ari watches me warily, as though he doesn't quite believe that I will let my questions go.

And I won't, forever. But I can certainly leave them for now.

IT'S BEEN hours since we tucked into either side of the large bed. The sponge is comfortable and cool. It taunts me with the sleep I could be getting if I could shut my mind off, even if just for a moment.

And if I could make myself stop fidgeting.

But I can't stop watching the rise and fall of his chest. I can't quell the rioting thoughts that fill my mind as I scan his bruised torso, following the bloody lines of his bandages.

Each time I move, I half-expect Ari's booming voice to order me to stop. But he seems just as unsettled as I am. Napo is the only one who has been able to find sleep, and I can't help but resent him for that.

Instead, my thoughts are coming to a boiling point, expanding and growing and bubbling over until I can't contain them anymore. I try to fortify my walls, to give Ari the quiet he needs to rest, instead of being forced to listen to my never-ending barrage of thoughts.

I can't stop thinking of all the death I have witnessed since I came here. Or how I contributed to the bloodshed. Or how close Ari was to being overtaken. How many warriors he fought and killed. How he had protected me, just like he promised. How fiercely I wanted to do the same.

That inevitably leads to thoughts about my sisters, wondering if they're safe.

Even Kane. Does he fight as well as Ari does? Will he be in danger, traveling alone, or was today only because I was the target?

"Kane is fine, Kala," Ari says. "And yes, you were the target."

I nod, having surmised as much. The assailants had clearly been trying to get around Ari to reach me. Since the king wants me, I can only imagine that either they are rebelling against their monarch, or they have a specific reason to want me dead.

"You aren't going to ask your hundred follow-up questions?" There is almost teasing in his tone.

"You wouldn't answer them if I did," I say.

My words are blunt, but there is no ire in my tone.

Still, Ari sighs.

"Couldn't, Kala. There's a difference."

Is that better? Worse? Certainly no less frustrating.

Turning over on my side, I meet Ari's sea-green eyes. And though he's only on the other side of the mattress, he might as well be an ocean away. Before I can wonder if it bothers him as much as it does me, a large, muscled arm stretches out, gripping my hip and pulling me toward him. Napo swims out of the way just in time, casting an irritable glance at us before settling onto the foot of the bed.

I can't even bring myself to feel bad for disturbing him, not when Ari tucks me into the crook of his arm, my face resting just beneath his chin and my body flush against his chest.

I expect it to set my nerves on fire the way his proximity usually does, but the warmth that spreads through me is more comforting than lustful this time.

"Peace, Kala." Though he directs the word to me, his own heartbeat slows to a steady, rhythmic thump in my ear.

Contentment emanates from behind the shields that

have slipped a little with each passing hour. Gradually, my thoughts fade to the back of my mind, peace flooding through my veins.

For the first time in what feels like ages, I fall into a deep, dreamless sleep.

CHAPTER EIGHTEEN

MELODI

I awake to an empty bed, but at least Ari doesn't bother telling me it can't happen again.

He doesn't say anything about it at all. Instead, he spends the day helping me practice my shields as we travel. Up and down. Up and down. Stronger. More finesse.

If I didn't already know he was tense about whatever awaits us at the palace, I would have figured it out when he doesn't so much as blink at the things leaking out when I let my shields drop entirely.

"Again," he orders.

And I comply. Apparently, there are some Mayima who are strong enough to break those walls down. Ari strongly hinted that the king is one of them, though he won't tell me any more about the enigmatic man who ordered my kidnapping.

So I practice harder while Ari tests the strength of my barriers, but the tension doesn't leave his features. He eyes me from his mount as we cross another sandbar and dive even farther down into the ocean's depths. "You need to keep your shields up any time you are not alone. Don't trust anyone at the palace."

I nod, trying not to be frustrated by the vague warning.

"You expect me to be in danger there, then?"

He gives me a calculating look, studying me for several moments before shaking his head irritably.

"I don't know what the king wants with you, but it's safe to assume you will be in danger one way or another. If not from him, then from those who seek to hurt him," he bites out the words.

I look away from him.

Does he realize how much information he has given me with that statement?

Of course he does. In the short time I've known him, I already gathered that Ari does nothing without purpose.

We resume practicing my shields after that until we get to our inn for the night. I try not to think too hard about our sleeping arrangements, but when we get in the bed for the night, Ari doesn't bother putting Napo between us.

It almost worries me more, after everything he's said. From what I have observed of him, Ari is not careless. He is not weak. So when he pulls me against his chest, I hear everything he isn't saying.

The goodbye he isn't giving me.

Not for the first time, I wonder what's going to happen when we get to the palace, where Ari will go when his mission is complete.

"Shields, Kala," he orders softly.

I put them up automatically, and approval emanates from him. He runs his thumb along my hipbone in a gesture that is both casual and possessive, and I'm not even sure he realizes he's doing it.

I'm glad my shields are up because there would be no hiding my reaction otherwise. As it is, he can probably hear my heart racing, feel it pound from my chest to his.

"King Cepheus is intelligent," he says suddenly.

At first I think he's responding to the questions I've tried not to ask all day. Then Ari goes on.

"Nothing escapes his notice," he warns. "And he does not tolerate weakness. He can't be led to believe there is… anything between us."

I tilt my head up to face Ari, trying and failing to ignore how close it puts my lips to his skin.

"Are you ever going to tell me what *is* between us?" My eyes meet his, and my heart thunders even faster, my blood rushing through my veins.

He doesn't deny it. He couldn't, not when his gaze is burning into mine like I am the sun itself and he has lived his entire life chained to the darkness.

"When I can." *If* I can, he means, but I don't push him. It's still better than *no*.

"Then answer one question for me."

He hesitates, and I don't wait for him to agree before I let slip the first real thing I ever wondered about him.

"Do you dream of my face too?"

Ari blinks, his hand freezing in its path up and down my side. The silence stretches out long enough that I begin to doubt he'll answer me at all. Still, I don't look away from his face. I can't.

If he tells me nothing else, I need to know this. That I'm not insane. That I'm not alone.

His features soften, and he pulls me tighter against him, tucking my head against his chest. When it comes, his answer is so quiet, I could almost believe that I imagined it but for the way it roots itself down into my very soul.

"Yes, Kala," he whispers. "I dream of you, too."

CHAPTER NINETEEN

MELODI

I carry Ari's words with me all morning, protecting them, shielding them in the recesses of my mind. It makes me feel less alone, hearing him willing to admit to this one thing.

I dream of you, too.

At least I'm not crazy. Whatever it is between us is real and tangible. And dangerous, if Ari is to be believed.

"We're nearly there." He interrupts my thoughts, pointing toward a glimmering tower in the distance.

The palace.

"Remember what I said." He doesn't need to expound further.

I have been doing nothing but considering his warnings all morning.

He spurs his marlin forward, mine eagerly following. His bandage is gone, his injury no more than a thin, barely discernible line. The Mayiman medicines seem to work even better than Madame's tonics.

As the palace grows larger, the capital city of Mayim

unfolding before us, warring thoughts tangle in my mind, like shells in a fisherman's net.

The streets are paved in brightly-colored stones, sparkling like polished gems that gleam and glitter as it winds toward the palace doors. The pearlescent city glows brightly, reflecting light from the bioluminescent plants and creatures that surround it.

But none of it compares to the breathtaking view of the palace itself.

I'm no stranger to opulence. Mother makes it into an artform, an obsession. What I didn't see in our own homes, I glimpsed from afar through the carriage windows on the trip from the harbor to the estate in Bondé. Sprawling mansions and elaborate castles. Luxurious chateaus with stained glass windows.

Not one of those places hold a candle to the palace in front of me.

Situated atop a brightly colored-coral reef, nine perfectly spiraling towers yawn toward the surface of the water, stretching and growing more narrow the higher up they go. And each of them are gilded—as if they've been dipped in liquid gold. It's the only color variation from the pearlescent walls coating the rest of the palace.

After the villages, I expected more noise. Maybe music. Crowded streets. In contrast, the capital looks almost abandoned.

The streets are silent, with impeccably manicured plant life. There is no garbage or debris. No loud voices. No children swimming around. Even the fish choose to swim around the city instead of through it. It's as if the ocean itself bends around this place, afraid to make any sudden movements. Afraid of drawing attention to itself.

Dread pools low in my stomach as we inch closer. Ari leads us up the main road, capturing the attention of the sparse crowds. The ones dressed as warriors respond to him the same way so many did on the way here—by making a fist and pounding it against their chest.

Others, dip their heads in respect, their curious gazes studying me. I do my best to keep my head down, refusing to meet their eyes, since mine draw too much attention. It isn't until we reach the palace gates that my attention snaps upward—toward the smell of death.

Floating near the doors, tethered only by chains holding them to the coral below, are cages. Each of them holds the body of a Mayima in various states of decay.

Two are nearly indistinguishable, barely more than bones. Spider crabs feast on what remains of their carcasses. Another cage is home to a fresh corpse, and the smell of death floating in the water around them is enough to make me gag.

And then my eyes land on the final cage. A woman with turquoise hair and lifeless silver eyes stares blankly ahead. Small silver fish gnaw at the place where one of her hands used to be. Green and purple bruises cover her beautiful golden brown skin, but that's not even the worst part.

The worst part is the small twitching in her leg and the silent tears streaming out from her eyes that tell me she's still alive.

It's not worse than anything Mother has done, even than what I have witnessed before. I should have been prepared to see such savagery displayed in such a beautiful place.

But it never gets less horrifying, seeing the kinds of things one person is willing to inflict on another. Bile rises in my throat just as Ari's voice sounds in my mind—an order and a reminder of what is to come.

"Walls, Kala."

I secure them into place, forcing the image of the girl out of my mind. Forcing myself to remember that there is so much more at stake. That I can't do anything for her.

After our pair of marlin are handed over to a waiting servant, Ari leads the way to our destination. He grows more distant and reserved the closer we draw to the palace.

It's quieter inside the palace and fear permeates the water around us—a living, tangible thing. We swim through brightly lit corridors, passing the bowed heads of servants and haughty nobles and warriors.

Not one of them dares to think louder than a whisper, if at all. Ari is similarly guarded, so I make sure that I am, too. Finally, Ari brings us to an imposing circular door, guarded by two massive guards—scowls permanently etched into their expressions.

I want to lean in closer to Ari, but I know that is impossible now. I would have sensed it even if he hadn't drilled it into my head.

Show no weakness in this place.

Give no hint of whatever strange connection is between us.

So, instead, I hold my head high, fixing my expression into something cold and impenetrable—a mirror of the one I have seen Zaina don so many times before. But when the doors finally open, my breathing falters.

I can't look at my surroundings. My gaze immediately flies to the man who awaits us perched on the throne which sits in the center of the room. I hadn't allowed myself to think about the king for too long, not wanting to get my hopes up only to have them dashed to pieces when reality set in. But the truth is impossible to avoid now.

King Cepheus is beautiful. Long, purple hair flows out from beneath a crown made of shells and gold, shining in stark contrast to his onyx skin. The soft curve of his nose, the sharp edges of his cheekbones and the slant of his brow are familiar, but it's his eyes that catch my attention.

Striking amethyst, a color I've only seen twice before.

On Mother. And in the mirror.

His gaze is cold as he assesses me, the way a predator looks at a small woodland creature that may or may not be worth the trouble of catching.

"Granddaughter. At last, you've come home."

CHAPTER TWENTY

MELODI

*G*randdaughter.

The king's granddaughter. The word *Kala* resounds in my head, and I know now for certain what it means. *Princess.*

Didn't some part of me suspect that all along? I just hoped it would be under different circumstances, a connection to someone who is not a monster. I can already tell that will not be the case with the king.

The girl in the cage would have told me that much. Then there is the feeling in the air like everyone in this palace is walking the edge of a knife like a tightrope, dead if they fall and bleeding even if they don't.

I never thought Ari was lying when he said the situation here would be dangerous, but when he overreacted to every sea creature that so much as looked at me along the journey, I lulled myself into a false sense of safety.

Dangerous. For both of us.

Standing before the king, Ari's words feel like an understatement. What would this man do with a weakness? Already, I have seen how he addresses disobedience, perceived or otherwise, and relationships between those of different classes is forbidden here.

Ari told me, and Kane reiterated it more than once in his sardonic way when I was still struggling to guard my thoughts about his cousin from him. So, I force myself to smile politely while he addresses Ari, while I make sands-damned sure that my shields are stronger than they've ever been.

"Well done, Commander Ariihau," the king praises the warrior with a nod of his head.

Ari bows with a fisted hand over his heart, and the gesture twists something inside of me. I don't like seeing him bow to anyone, I realize, let alone this man.

"Thank you, King Cepheus." Ari emphasizes the name just a bit, probably for my benefit.

Probably to remind me I need to respond. If Mother has no tolerance for insolence, I can safely assume the same is true for the king. A tentacle wraps around my ankle, and Napo gently prods me to address my grandfather, as if he, too, is concerned about the outcome of this meeting.

The king tracks the movement with a calculating gaze, but doesn't appear to mind Napo's presence.

"Thank you, King Cepheus," I echo, opening my shields just the barest amount.

I can do this. I have watched my sisters play this game with Mother for years. If they can shut down their expressions, I can certainly shut off my inner thoughts. Besides, if I can endure Damian's hands on my skin

111

without belying my revulsion, I can handle a conversation.

The king gives me a smile edged with condescension, and alarm bells go off in my head.

Not good enough. My shields are falling short, just as Ari warned me they would.

"Thank you, Commander Ariihau, for bringing her back to me." There is no warmth in his words, but I suspect there never is.

Ari bows again before turning on his heel to stride away. I wonder if I imagine the hesitation from him, the barest hint of panic, or if it is merely a projection of my own emotions.

For all I have envisioned getting to the palace, I hadn't considered that he might leave me once we arrived.

"Commander," King Cepheus' voice is an order, and Ari freezes in place. "You are not dismissed. We still have business."

Ari apologizes, and it stirs something inside of me, something primal and protective.

I can't afford to think about it anymore with the king scrutinizing my every expression, though, so I clear my mind.

If I don't have perfect shields, at least I can control my thoughts. I examine the room, focusing on the innocuous details—like the pale blue light that glows from the bioluminescent lanterns. The way my grandfather raps his fingers against the arm of his chair, just like Mother always does.

The delicate throne at his side sits empty. Was it for

my mother? My grandmother? Is the king's wife still alive?

I feel the weight of my grandfather's stare, and I turn back expectantly to hear what it is that has brought me to him; what he wants from me. He is all but glowing with satisfaction, an expression so eerily reminiscent of my mother that it sends a chill down my spine.

He rises from his throne, picking up his trident from where it rests on the ground and sheathing it in a practiced motion. It is ornate to the point of being ostentatious, gilded and encrusted with jewels, but no less deadly for its excess.

Swimming artfully to my side, he waves a hand in the direction of the chamber door.

"It's been a long journey, Melodi." I try not to react to his use of my name. Or question how he learned it, and how long he's been watching me. "You must want to rest." There is no inflection in his tone and I wonder if this is a test.

Will it show weakness on my part if I agree? Will it be a challenge if I don't?

I think about Mother, and how everything with her is a challenge of some sort. A game. A way for her to study you, to understand you, to find inventive ways to exploit you. I fight the urge to look to Ari for answers.

"As you wish, my king," I say, dipping my head respectfully.

He arches a violet eyebrow, the corner of his full lips quirking up in amusement, or approval, I can't tell.

"Grandfather," he corrects.

My pulse quickens as he leads me out of the room, Ari following close behind.

It's an effort to keep up as he escorts us down several halls and up one of the spiral towers. He's watching me, taking me in as we go, and I can't help but compare him to his daughter. I have seen rare glimpses of warmth from Mother, but something tells me that is more than anyone has seen from the king.

"All these years, and I never thought to look on land," he remarks. "Clever girl, my Ursula."

The words are more of a curse than a compliment.

I try to calm my racing pulse, and once again, gently reinforce my mental walls, sealing them tightly so that no stray thought can escape. When I remain silent he turns his head to better assess me.

"And you?" The question feels like another test, and I'm not at all sure if it's one I will pass this time.

"I am nothing like my mother." It's a truth that will quickly be discovered, so I might as well admit it.

A slow smile stretches his lips, tugging at his beard.

"Good," he draws out the word and I resist the urge to back away. "Your mother was too soft."

Was?

He speaks of her like she's dead. Does he want her to be? Is he planning to kill her?

I wonder if I would grieve her, in spite of all the things she's done and the lives she's destroyed. I hope that I would, that I haven't lost the humanity I have spent a lifetime clinging to in the wake of her cruelty.

I start to tell him that I hadn't experienced a side of

Mother that was too soft, but compared to him, I doubt that's true.

My silence doesn't seem to bother him. If anything, I get the feeling he prefers it when he dips his head.

"Perhaps it's a good thing she took you when she did. I might have disposed of you before you could be of use to me." There's a note of regret in his tone, like he is disappointed in himself for nearly passing up whatever opportunity he sees in me.

Not for his willingness to murder a baby, of course. It's clear he has exactly zero qualms about that.

"Whatever she took clearly made you defective, too," he adds after a moment, his narrowed gaze assessing me.

Too?

Is he referring to the human side of me? Or does he know it's something else? The way I can't speak on land.

"We will have you inspected first thing in the morning to make sure there aren't any other obvious deficiencies."

I wish I could say that the words sting, but they're said in the cold, practical tone that Mother has used all of my life. Not an insult as much as an observation.

I want to ask what plans he has for me, how I can possibly be useful to him, but I suspect he won't answer. More than that, I suspect he will punish me for asking.

So I stay silent. He does as well until we stop at the end of the corridor, just outside of a round, bronze door.

"This is the entrance to your chambers. I'll leave you here for the night."

Unless my sense of time is completely skewed, it's barely late afternoon, and I'm already being locked away for the night. Another test? Or merely a display of power? My answer is the same, regardless.

"Of course." I dip my head in assent. "Good evening, King Cepheus."

"Grandfather," he corrects again.

Though his tone is mild, his expression isn't. It tells me his next correction won't be nearly so gentle.

"Good evening, Grandfather," I say obediently.

His grin becomes almost feral as he turns to Ari. My heart stops, my limbs weakening with an unexpected wave of panic. Ari doesn't look my way, but his fingers twitch, like he's trying to tell me to stay calm. So I force myself to inhale, exhale.

"Commander," the king says. "As a reward for bringing my granddaughter home unharmed, I give you the honor of being her personal guard. I trust that you will continue to keep her safe."

Relief that he will be close wars with unease at my grandfather's slightly-too-pleased expression. Perhaps this is only his magnanimous face, the one he wears when he bestows favors rather than agony upon his subjects.

If Ari is concerned, he gives no sign of it. His shields are more firmly in place than I've ever felt them. It leaves me feeling strangely empty, unmoored. He places his fist to his chest, bowing his head in response.

"On my honor," he says evenly.

"You may have your things brought to your new chambers," Cepheus says, gesturing to the door next door to mine.

With that, the king shuts the door behind me, closing me into my new prison. There's no sound of a lock clicking into place, but that doesn't surprise me. Mother never locked the doors to keep us inside. She kept us there with pure fear.

This must be where she learned it.

For all that I chose to come here, or at least chose to come without a fight, I didn't consider the permanence of that decision. There was always danger, but it didn't occur to me until now that I might be trapped here for the rest of my life.

I suppose I can't complain, though. Even knowing what I do now, I couldn't have chosen any other way. The visceral part of me that dreams of Ari and feels his pain and needs his touch could not be persuaded to leave him.

Besides, my gilded cage is certainly preferable to the ones outside.

CHAPTER TWENTY-ONE

ARIIHAU

I should be relieved.

It would have been markedly harder to keep Kala safe if the king had put me on a different assignment. And not keeping her safe hasn't been an option from the moment she appeared in my dreams.

For all that she's made a joke of it, she's been in danger from the moment Kane pulled her into the sea. I don't know yet what the king wants from her, but I do know it can't be good. Nothing about him is good, least of all his intentions.

I do know what the rebels want, however. They want her dead.

That's not something I will allow to happen, even if it means taking out the warriors I've worked beside for half my life. I want a new regime as badly as they do, but not at the expense of her life.

Nothing is worth that to me.

Napo pushes me toward the bed and I don't argue, even though it takes everything in me not to open the door to Kala's room and drag her onto the mattress next to me.

Again, I recognize that I should be feeling some relief at my new assignment. The calling would have been almost unbearable if I had been forced to sleep in the barracks. As her guard, at least there will be only one wall that separates us instead of an entire palace.

Which will be a mixed bag, if she can't keep her seas-damned thoughts to herself. It will be funny when I have worked so hard to survive only to be driven to insanity by one harmless *not-quite-mayima*.

Still, the benefits should outweigh the risks. *Should*. But something in King Cepheus' calculating gaze stops me from feeling even the barest hint of relief.

What game is he playing? Does he know the truth about the rebellion, or my connection to his heir? Does he suspect it?

I was raised in the palace, as all Warrior children are, trained under the commanders here while my parents were stationed far enough away that they were at no risk of making me soft. Not that it would have been much of a risk, considering they are both Warriors themselves, through and through.

So, I am intimately familiar with the barbarity of our king, the way he always knows more than he lets on. I grew up under his watchful gaze, saw the punishments he doled out just because he could.

Kala's shields are weak, compared to most Mayima her age, and the king's powers of perception are strong, even without breaking the mind barrier. Even now, I can hear her thoughts on the other side of the door, questioning everything around her with the insatiable kind of curiosity that will get her killed here. So it wouldn't be a stretch that she let something slip.

I slam my shields more firmly into place, though every part of me rebels at the separation. We can't afford mistakes right now, though. Not when the king has motives I can't guess at.

The only comfort I have is that he has no need to play games with us. Even if he garnered more than she meant for him to, he may have just dismissed it as the silly crush of a young girl.

We can hope, anyway. Because if he knows the truth… I shake my head, dismissing the thought as quickly as it came.

If he knew the truth, he would already have destroyed us both.

CHAPTER TWENTY-TWO

MELODI

*T*here is a second door in my chambers.

Even if Cepheus hadn't said that Ari was staying next door, I would have known who was on the other side. I can feel his presence through the walls.

I lean against the door, absently playing with a piece of seaweed left over from my journey here. Before I know what I'm doing, I've separated it into several pieces. My fingers go through the motions of twisting and braiding memorials for the bodies we passed in cages outside.

I think again of the girl who is still alive, wondering how much longer until she shares their fate. I picture the defeat in her eyes, the stillness of her limbs.

Then I make one for her too.

I stay near the door for longer than I should. It's silent on the other side. No movement to track, no thoughts that I can hear. So I focus on my room, at least in part to keep from going mad.

Each glimmering wall is just as glamorous as the rest of the palace. Woven rugs made of kelp and algae line the floors, feeling as plush beneath my bare feet as the fur ones back home.

A giant clamshell rests against the center wall. The iridescent mother of pearl headboard refracts the light from the shimmering lanterns, casting the room in a soft, hazy glow. The oversized sponge mattress and pillows practically beg me to climb into them, whispering false promises of the sleep I know I won't find.

At least, not alone.

There is a vanity with various shells and jewels. A closet full of the most extravagant gowns I've seen since being pulled into the water.

Are they intended for me? Or did this room belong to someone else? My mother, perhaps?

Along the walls are gilded shelves with books made from what appears to be blubber and some sort of refined seaweed. I flip through them. Some are full of Mayiman history, others appear to be adventures or love stories. Most of them are in the common tongue, but a few are much older, written in an ancient, pictorial language.

With nothing else to do, I choose one about the lore of the Great Sea Dragon. There is no name on the first page, no hint of who it belongs to, or where it came from, but the pages are more worn than the others, several of them marked or dogeared.

I scan through the first few chapters, greedily soaking up the information. I hadn't even realized that dragons still existed, let alone that they were linked to the royal families.

Damian said he encountered one with Zaina, that it nearly killed him.

I wish it had. Or, at the very least, that Mother had made him keep the scars so he was as hideous on the outside as he was inside.

I wonder how he reacted to my absence. Is he sad, in whatever way he is capable of? Frantic because he has been robbed of the next closest thing to being blood related to Mother? Furious, and taking it out on the servant girls?

Those musings inevitably lead to thoughts of my mother. I have no idea how she feels at my absence either. She certainly doesn't miss me, when she went to such great lengths to avoid me. But is she worried?

Is worry a thing that she feels?

She has always been an enigma to me, a contrast of cruelty and protectiveness, of practicality and excess. Though obsession with opulence certainly makes more sense now, if she grew up surrounded by all of this. Perhaps in this very room, reading this book about dragons.

I wonder if she misses her home. If that's why she is never far from the sea, why she continues to go by *Ursula* when she could have changed her name.

Shutting out thoughts of home, I turn the page. The next page is marked with ink. Sentences and entire paragraphs are circled or underlined multiple times.

Each kingdom was blessed with a dragon....their loyalty to the monarchy is absolute. ...bond will shift as the royal line does.

More questions churn in my mind, and I add them to the list of things I'll likely never have the answers to.

Hours pass before I finally climb into bed, and still sleep eludes me.

AFTER WHAT FEELS LIKE AN ETERNITY, a knock finally sounds at my door.

It must be morning—something that is even harder to distinguish in the dark waters of my room. A moment later, the pale blue head of a servant girl appears in the frame.

"Come in," I call with my mind, and she dips her head low before closing the door behind her.

She doesn't say anything, her mind completely closed off as she rests a tray on the end of my bed. Her cautious golden gaze avoids mine at all cost.

It's a good reminder to shield my thoughts as well. The servants back home weren't allowed to speak with us, and they were under strict orders to report any suspicious behavior to Mother.

Maybe it's the same here.

While she disappears into my closet, I examine the tray and what seems to be the Mayiman equivalent to coffee or tea. Or so I assume.

There is a clear carafe filled with small jellies. When I remove the lid, a few of them escape, and I test the feeling of one between my fingers. It bursts with little pressure, liquid pooling out into the water in front of me.

I dart my tongue out to taste it. It's rich, with hints of lavender and honey and cream. I pour a few more into my mouth, popping them with my tongue and savoring each one like a sip of tea.

I've already finished most of the carafe by the time the girl emerges again, carrying a long turquoise gown.

Another knock sounds at the door, and she hangs the dress near the mirror before turning to answer it. She moves back, dipping her head respectfully as an aged Mayiman man sweeps into the room. He coldly explains that he needs to examine me.

Examine me?

Some of the king's words come back to mind—*we will have you inspected... no other deficiencies...*

He instructs me to lie down, and I oblige after only a short hesitation. He pokes and prods at every inch of my skin.

"Soft," he mutters, reminding me of when Ari said it.

But this man is cold. Clinical. He says it like he's pronouncing a death sentence, and fear trickles through my limbs.

Next, he tests the reflexes in my joints, which are also not to his liking. Finally, there is an internal examination that makes my skin crawl. I think only of my shields rather than his invasive touch. Ari is just on the other side of the wall.

If he hears me, he will come in here.

The thought is both a comfort and a deterrent. Not only do I not particularly want him in here for the overly intimate examination, I know how dangerous his intervention would be.

But it is a comfort, also, remembering his muscled form as he held the line of the attacking rebels, the resolution in his voice when he told me he would never let me die.

Not even if the king willed it, was his unspoken promise.

Finally, the man is done, declaring that I'm not barren and therefore the servant—Moli—can continue with her assistance. He's gone before I can ask him what would have happened if I was barren.

"It would mean that you could not inherit, as Kala'ni Danica cannot."

My gaze snaps up to meet Moli's. Whatever she sees in my expression has fear creeping up into hers.

"Apologies, Kala. I—I didn't mean to speak out of turn. I thought you were asking—"

I curse myself for not securing my walls enough, firmly locking them in place before I respond.

"No, it's fine. Really," I say, and she relaxes a little. "Thank you, for telling me."

She stares at me curiously before nodding, and I wonder if anyone has ever thanked her before.

I want to ask her about Kala'ni Danica, but I don't want to get her in trouble. Still, I feel a small sense of victory when a tiny, hesitant smile appears on her lips, and she gestures for me to follow her into the bathing chamber.

Perhaps I don't have answers, but I have someone who might someday be willing to provide them. And at least I don't have to be yet another source of fear in her life.

CHAPTER TWENTY-THREE

MELODI

*M*oli is quiet as she works, scrubbing my skin with a gray stone and white sand until I am polished—my skin more smooth than it has ever been in my life. Next, she pulls the leaves off of a few flowers on the wall, squeezing them until a creamy pink oil appears, one that reminds me of the tiare flowers on the island.

She rubs it into my skin and hair until my curls are manageable and the rest of me is soft and shiny. Once she's satisfied with her work, she carefully twists my curls into submission, adorning my head with a pearl-studded circlet, before dressing me in the gown.

The top is two loosely connected triangles, made of something golden and shimmery. The skirt is fitted, made of the same material and just long enough to restrict my movements.

It feels intentional, a reminder that I am merely ornamental to the king's needs.

The outfit is overall less revealing than the netting

was, but still displays far more skin than I'm used to showing. Moli is just securing the last clasp in place when another knock sounds at the door.

"Kala, the king awaits." Ari's voice wraps around my thoughts, soothing, like the finest silk.

Her hands falter for a moment and I'm not sure if it's in response to his voice or my thought, but I secure my walls once again.

"Thank you," I think, sincerely. She dips her head once in response.

"You're welcome, Kala." With that, she's exiting the room, and I am once more face to face with Ari.

It's an effort not to reach out and touch him, to remind myself of the way his skin feels against my palms, the heartbeat that thunders in his chest to a tune that has become so familiar.

"Walls, Kala," Ari reminds me, his voice a shadow of a whisper, but an order nonetheless.

Despite his words, I can sense the relief flooding through him, a mirror of what I feel. And for now, that's enough. It has to be.

At least, that's what I tell myself as I secure my shields and try to focus on anything else. The pale, gleaming walls. The light drifting in through the open windows. The sound of whales in the distance.

I can't be sure, but the pull between us feels even stronger than before, like a spring coiling back together after it's been pulled taut. A muscle clenches in his jaw as he surveys me through his thick lashes.

"The king's healer visited."

"He did," I confirm, watching Ari closely.

His Adam's apple dips and his taut jaw twitches. "You had your walls up."

"Per your instructions," I remind him. It wasn't really an experience I felt like sharing. Particularly not with him.

He glares to show me what he thinks of me being cheeky about it.

"Did he hurt you?" Ari growls out each word, and I shake my head.

"No," I assure him. "He was very clinical."

Ari nods, a sharp jerk of his chin. "If he had—"

"I know," I tell him.

And I do.

If the healer had hurt me, he would not survive this day, whatever the consequences of that were. Perhaps I should be bothered by that, but Ari's protection feels wholly different from Mother's and Damian's. More like that of my sisters.

Deadly, yes, but not needlessly cruel.

A rush of water and shadow swims between us and Napo appears in front of Ari, his expression incredulous. Two tentacles rest against his body as if he's a human with his hands on his hips. It's enough of a distraction, one I am wildly grateful for, that I can't help but laugh.

"You were still sleeping," Ari says in answer to whatever unspoken question the octopus posed.

Napo only narrows his eyes further, swimming ahead of us with irritation rolling off of him in waves. We catch up with him just outside of the dining hall.

The octopus swims over the heads of the warriors guarding the door. They barely acknowledge him, their attention fixed on their commander instead. But they don't stop him either. They raise a fist in a familiar gesture before allowing us to pass.

"Granddaughter," the king's voice booms, silencing the clinking of cutlery. "Join me."

It isn't a request.

All eyes are fixed on us as we pass table after table of nobles and servants rushing between them. The room is uncomfortably silent. Not a single stray thought escapes even the youngest Mayima, making me even more aware of my inadequacies with my mental shields.

Ari leads me to the head table, pulling out the empty chair next to Cepheus for me to sit in. As soon as I take it, he pushes it back toward the table before taking his place as sentry on the wall behind me.

"I trust you slept well," the king says, his eyes barely leaving the plate in front of him.

He spears a bite of thinly sliced raw fish, scooping a mound of shredded green seaweed onto his fork before returning it to his mouth.

"The room was lovely, Grandfather," I say politely, and he grins.

I wonder at the king's good mood. And the fact that the guests are well into their meals by the time I arrived. Did he want me to be late? To parade me in front of them? Is this something he will punish me for? Or worse, Ari...

I don't follow the thought any further and instead clear my mind of anything relevant as a plate is set before me. I'm barely into my third bite of the surprisingly delicious seaweed salad when commotion pulls our attention to the main door.

The woman from the cage is escorted through by Kane and another Mayiman warrior. Her eyes are hollow as she meets the king's gaze, but her expression is hardened. Unafraid.

My stomach drops as they drag her to our table.

"Ah, Natia," the king says, casually sitting back in his chair. "So glad you could find the time to join us."

His lips twitch with amusement, and the rest of the room laughs uncomfortably. The girl only stares mutely ahead.

"It would appear that you told the truth about my daughter." Something flashes in her eyes, something defiant, but not a single thought escapes her mind as he continues. "Because of this, I have decided to set you free, despite your daring to interfere on behalf of one of the *humans*." He spits the word like a curse, erasing any doubt as to how he feels about my people.

The people that used to be mine.

All this because she helped a human? Is getting a message to them considered the same as helping? Surely not, when there are Mayiman traders. Then again, the king is hardly reasonable.

A moment passes, charged like the air just before lightning strikes.

"Is that why you have decided to let me go?" she asks quietly, something like a challenge in her tone. "Because of my information?"

Something passes between them that I can't quite read, a rare moment of real emotion flitting over the king's features, more than offense, but not quite grief. His right hand goes to cover his left, an odd urgency in the movement.

The smallest corner of her mouth tilts up in a wan, bitter smile, and he scowls.

Then his expression clears, and he casually dismisses her with a wave of his hand. It would be casual, anyway, if we hadn't all just witnessed their exchange. Not that anyone is brave enough to acknowledge it.

Natia eyes the king with unveiled disgust before turning to follow the guards out of the room.

Including Kane. There is no trace of the man who teased and joked on the way here. He reminds me of my sisters, trapped in a life of violence when he is capable of so much more.

My thoughts cut off as a strange sensation takes over me. It's subtle at first—a shiver of cold. A whisper of touch along the walls of my mind. Goosebumps trail up my neck and over my scalp as tendrils of ice creep down my spine.

My pulse quickens, and I reinforce my shields once again. The gentle tug comes from the left, and I wonder if it's my grandfather testing me, poking and prodding around in my head, trying to read my thoughts. But the pull comes from farther away, and I have a strong feeling that his touch would not be so benign.

I scan the long table, under the guise of reaching for my goblet, my gaze lingering on each face until I find the source. A face so familiar that it haunts my waking nightmares. Violet eyes stare back at me, into me... The resemblance is so striking that I am momentarily frozen in place.

She subtly dips her head before returning to her quiet conversation with the man at her side.

A cousin? A sister? Mother herself?

The possibilities run wild in my head, choking out all rational thought. Obviously, I know it's not her. It can't be. And she feels... Different. But still, I can only barely fight the urge to swim as far away as possible.

"What are you looking at, child?" Cepheus' voice pulls my attention back to the moment.

"Apologies, Grandfather. I thought—" I trail off when he glances down the table, his lips pursing in response.

"I see," he says, and I wonder if he does.

If he understands the fear that his daughter has instilled in her children. But of course he does. He is the monster who created the monster who raised me.

"Who is she?" I ask carefully, setting down my glass with trembling fingers.

"That is Danica," he replies dismissively. "Your mother's twin sister."

CHAPTER TWENTY-FOUR

ARIIHAU

*A*fter breakfast, I escort Kala to the library for etiquette lessons with her aunt.

The fear was palpable when we first arrived, but after some brief conversation, the set of her shoulders is more relaxed, and her panic has eased. She's still not comfortable with Kala'ni, but she's not as afraid as she was before.

Danica isn't her father. She isn't cruel, though I wouldn't consider her exactly *kind* either. Her father keeps her alive because she offers no threat to him, quietly agreeing when he declares her unfit for marriage, accepting the honorific he mockingly placed on her name. 'Ni is usually to denote a married woman, but Cepheus declared that she was as good as married for all that she was available.

The only reason she's lived this long is because she keeps her head down, something I hope she can teach her niece to do.

I doubt anyone would be stupid enough to attack her here, so publicly, and I've made sure there were ample warnings to anyone who might consider it. So I should feel safe enough standing here, waiting for the inevitable arrival of my cousin. Still my jaw clenches, the muscles in my arms straining against the desire to move closer, the primal need to protect her.

Fortunately, Kane shows up only an hour after we arrive. His face is carved into a cold mask, even moreso than being back at the palace would normally account for. It's easy to forget sometimes that he is several decades my senior, but today he seems to carry every one of those years on his shoulders.

"I need to request leave. It's time for me to visit home," he says without preamble.

"Your home in Bondé?" I ask, my low tone matching his.

There's a subtle hint of sarcasm that only he will catch.

No one is around, but it's still best to be as discreet as we can. He doesn't bother to look surprised that I know what he really wants is to escort Natia back to her home.

He's always had a soft spot for the quirky Mayima who harbors an insatiable curiosity about humans. This is hardly the first time she has joined the ranks of people he has had to watch hurt by the king—has had to personally escort to be hurt by the king.

But it never gets easier, for any of us.

"That's the one," he confirms.

"I'll grant you leave to visit your parents," I tell him.

I'll cover for you, I'm saying.

"But I need you to make an additional stop," I add.

Kala was trying not to think about it for most of breakfast, but of course, I hear her better than most. She's worried about her sisters, and worried I'll have no way to make good on the deal I made her now that Natia was tortured for doing not much more.

I don't want to ask my cousin to take this risk, but I gave her my word, and there's no one else I trust as much. Besides, he'll already be there.

"The sisters?" Kane asks, already knowing where I'm headed.

I raise an eyebrow.

"They're the ones she helped," he says, not quite an explanation.

I know instinctively that he's talking about a different *she* now. Natia.

I can't help but marvel at the irony of Kala's sisters being the reason she was found—or that Kala'ni Ursula was, anyway.

If Natia hadn't spotted Ursula, I would never have found Kala. She would still be in the hands of Damian— the vile man who dared to touch her and believe that she belonged to him.

My fists clench at my sides, my blood pounding in my veins.

"Easy," Kane cautions.

I take a breath, clearing my features of the rage that had been overtaking me. Kala looks over, and I quickly rein back the emotion I inadvertently let seep into her consciousness.

"How do you know Natia is the one who helped?" I ask, reverting to the topic at hand when Kala returns her attention to her aunt.

"It might have escaped your notice, but Kala is not so

great at controlling her thoughts," he says, his tone a bit lighter than it was when he came in. "I heard more than I needed to about her sisters and where they might be in the day we traveled together. For that matter, I heard more than I needed to about *everything*."

I glare at him, but it doesn't deter him.

"Not that I haven't often admired the defined ridges of your muscles myself. Or the way your eyes gleam in the wan shafts of sunlight. Or the way your very skin sparkles with the luster of a thousand—"

"Are you quite finished?" I cut him off.

Kane shrugs, an imitation of his usual smirk tugging at his lips. "I hadn't even gotten to her reactions."

I give him a flat look. "Don't."

"You don't want to hear about how heat surges through—?" he trails off meaningfully.

Shaking my head, I sigh. "You should probably get going if you want to leave quietly."

His face darkens again, and I instantly regret stealing his much-needed moment of levity, even if it was at my expense.

"Are you ever going to tell me what's going on there?" he asks, gesturing to Kala.

I don't bother to hedge. "You already know."

He looks away. "I was hoping I was wrong."

"You aren't," I tell him bluntly.

A few of the nobles swim past, their haughty expressions narrowing on us in suspicion. Kane stretches and leans back against the wall, pretending to study one of the books on the shelves.

"Great," he says once they're gone, his tone dripping

with sarcasm. "Shall I just start torturing you myself, then? Or would you prefer to wait for our king's gentle touch?"

"I have it under control," I lie.

Nothing feels remotely controlled where she's concerned.

"Sure you do," he says with a shake of his head. "Well I should be off. Kindly send word if I should expect to come home to your severed limbs rotting in a cage. You know I like to be prepared."

"I'm not sure how you'd like me to convey that message from said cage," I respond in an equally nonchalant tone. "But I'll certainly do my best."

"Have Napo bring a note," he suggests, and I roll my eyes.

Then, his expression turns more genuine and he places a hand on my shoulder, the closest thing to affection Mayima show one another.

"Just be careful, Cousin."

I nod curtly. "And you as well. Tell the family I said hello."

"Consider your message delivered."

He swims away as quickly as he had come, and I try not to wonder if the next time we see each other, there will be bars in between us.

One way or the other.

CHAPTER TWENTY-FIVE

MELODI

*K*ala'ni Danica is nothing like my mother. She is reserved and cautious. While there is still an iciness that coats her words, she is not as cold as her sister or her father, which is a relief in itself. By the time my lessons are over, though, she seems just as eager to escape the library as I am.

Once we're safely behind my doors, I let my shields down more than I've allowed myself to all day. My stomach growls as my gaze rakes over the tray of food on the bed. I don't wait before helping myself to some of the seaweed wrapped scallops.

Ari doesn't leave right away like I was expecting. Instead, he shifts closer, and the proximity warms me from the inside out.

When he speaks though, it's not what I was expecting him to say.

"Kane is getting word to your sisters."

A curious mix of relief and dread settles over me.

I don't know how I feel about Kane, but he obviously

means a lot to Ari, and I can't handle the idea of anyone getting hurt because of me. Images of the woman with her missing hand assault me, and I force them out of my mind.

Mother may well do worse to my sisters if they go to Delphine for me. So I don't argue, don't ask him to call Kane back.

Perhaps I am more my mother's daughter than I realize. Or perhaps fear turns us all into monsters.

Either way, the food turns to ash in my mouth.

Ari gives me an inscrutable look, and I wonder how many of those thoughts he's heard. If he thinks less of me for them.

"Peace, Kala," he says. "We all do what we must in order to protect the people we love."

It's a small comfort, but a comfort nonetheless. One I desperately cling to in the days to come.

THOUGH MY TIME is ostensibly filled with lessons, meals, and tours of the palace, there's an ominous feeling in each of my grandfather's assessing glances, like the tenuous calm just before a hurricane lands.

I haven't forgotten my questions—about my mother, my father, my bond with Ari. Neither am I foolish enough to think that chasing answers is an easy risk to take. Ari's warning resounds in my head with each interaction.

Don't trust anyone at the palace.

So, I don't. I keep my head down, gleaning what I can

from every interaction while desperately trying to keep my shields in place.

Even though he swims with me to each summons, each meal, each lesson, and sleeps just on the other side of my bedroom wall, I find myself missing Ari more and more. It's beginning to drive me mad. This constant restlessness, the call to go to him that I cannot answer makes it impossible to sleep.

To eat.

To breathe.

"How are your lessons coming along, Melodi?" My grandfather's voice rips me from my spiraling thoughts, and I check my shields.

Relief trickles in. They are firmly in place.

"They are going well, Grandfather." I force a smile, and he nods.

After breakfast this morning, the king leads my tour of the palace. Ari follows us at a distance, and I try not to look back at him or think of him at all.

Cepheus leads us into a private room that reminds me of a museum. Or maybe a graveyard. Giant statues line the floor, carved from some type of pristine, glowing white stone. There are warriors and kings and queens, but they're not what catch my eye.

Instead, my attention is fixed on the massive sculpture of a serpent that winds around the room. It has four legs, two at either end of its elongated body. Scales line its back like daggers. Gleaming eyes stare out beneath a scaled brow. Fire streams from a gaping mouth with hundreds of sharp teeth.

I think back to the book in my room about the Great

Dragon, wondering if this is the creature it was referring to, if it's out there, somewhere still.

"I'm glad," the king responds, pulling my attention away from the statue. "You seem to be settling into life here well. Better than I expected, considering that you were taken from here."

I swallow hard. It's a risk, but it's the closest thing he's given me to an opening since I arrived.

"I wish I knew what happened that made her leave," I say, and his violet eyes turn to stone, his fists clenching in front of him.

"Melodi," he warns, his tone cutting like a sharpened knife through butter.

I dip my head respectfully, just as I have each time before. He tilts his head to the side, his calculating gaze studying me. Then he sighs with something close to indulgence—feigned, of course.

"She was weak," he answers my question flatly. "And she didn't know her place."

Her place to be an ornament, to do his bidding without complaint.

"Then again, none of the children learned that lesson particularly well," he goes on, running a hand over the glowing trident of some former king. "Except Danica, and of course, she is all but useless otherwise."

"Where are they now?" I know I'm pushing my luck, but I'm so deeply curious about what other family I may have.

I've assumed his heir is in a different estate, or perhaps visiting the villages. When I see a cold, cruel smile pass his lips, I realize how very naive that assumption was.

His eyes glint when they lock onto mine. "They're dead. They either killed each other or exhausted their usefulness to me."

My stomach sinks.

It's not just the statement that stops me short, it's the tone and the delivery. The casual manner he dons when referencing the deaths of his family. His children. It sounds so much like something Mother would say.

And why did they kill each other? For the throne? For something else?

"Our leadership here is not as weak as the human world. Only the strongest will inherit."

A sudden, hollow feeling encompasses me. If his heirs are gone, and Danica can't inherit...

This is why he has kept me alive. For now.

As much as I want to be grateful that I am *useful* to him, there is no part of me that wants to inherit a savage throne, covered in the blood of his children. I don't want to be considered worthy to take up that mantle, or to do whatever it is he thinks I'll need to do to earn it.

More than that, I know now for certain that I will be a captive for the rest of my life.

He will never let me go.

CHAPTER TWENTY-SIX

MELODI

*T*he revelation that Cepheus intends for me to be queen someday haunts me for the rest of the day.

It follows me through my lessons with Danica. Through dinner. Through my introductions to several noblemen whose infuriating, leering stares aren't even enough to pull me from the moroseness of my thoughts.

I swim to my room amongst the ghosts of all the children he's murdered. Ari is silent as the grave beside me as he shuts the door, leaving me to the solitude of my room —this room I believed was my mother's. It could have belonged to any of them.

I move my gaze to the door that connects my room to Ari's. My swaying feet carry me across the room until I'm floating right in front of it, my fingers tracing the grooves of the smooth sandstone before coming to rest on the glimmering handle.

It has never been opened, and it's taking everything in me not to burst through it right now. To fall into his arms, to cling to him and take whatever comfort I can wrangle from his touch.

A knock on the main door has me swimming away to float in the center of the room—as far from Ari's door as I can manage. A heartbeat later, Moli enters with a bowed head. Her pale blue hair streams out around her as she moves forward, never once meeting my eyes.

We silently go through the motions as she helps me undress, bathe and redress in my short nightgown. She hesitates at the door, her golden eyes drifting up to meet mine.

"Is there anything else I can do for you, Kala?" There is genuine concern in her tone.

My mood must worry her. Offering her a gentle smile, I shake my head.

"No, thank you, Moli."

She dips her head, before leaving me alone once again.

It's too silent in the room. Too loud in my head.

Hours pass as I swim the length of the room, back and forth, back and forth, slowly drowning in the oceans of my mind. I haven't even registered my hand on the door-knob until I'm pushing it open.

Ari's eyes lock onto mine from the center of the room. His jaw is clenched, his hands in fists at his sides, and it looks like he's been pacing too. The relief is almost instantaneous. Without the walls between us, just having him in my line of sight...it feels like I can stop holding my breath.

But I want more. I need more. I need *him*.

"Go back to your rooms, Kala," he says gruffly, his muscles going rigid.

"I can't sleep."

"I know." He runs a hand through the teal strands of his hair, his shoulders slumping as he echoes the words. "I know."

I hesitantly shift closer, my toes grazing the seaweed rug next to his bed. The blankets are undisturbed and I wonder if he even tried to rest. Another shift forward and another, until I am barely a breath away.

The heat from his body melts into me, and my eyelids flutter in response. I can hear his heartbeat thundering against his chest, syncing with mine already. When I meet his emerald gaze, it hardens into something more resigned.

"But, you will sleep better alone than you would if the king found you in my room," he adds.

Guilt and shame crash over me in waves. If the king found me in Ari's room, perhaps I wouldn't sleep that night, but Ari would likely be dead. The thought tears at my fragile control.

"I'm sorry. I'm so sorry. I'll go." Tears pool from my eyes, mingling with the saltwater around us, and there is nothing I can do to stop them.

I turn to go before he can make this worse, but he reaches out to stop me. One solid arm wraps around me, and then another, pulling my back against his chest. He buries his face in my hair, cradling me like I am the most precious thing in the world to him.

"I am sorry, Kala. I wish I could explain, but I need you to trust me that it won't be this way forever," he says. "Can you do that?"

I nod, and he lets go, leaving me with that strangely

empty feeling once more. But the bit of contact soothed the panicked ache that had been working its way through me before.

It won't be this way forever.

Does that mean that we won't always have to be apart? Or that we won't have this connection forever?

Would it be worse, feeling this horrible, endless longing with him on the other side of the door for the rest of my life or not having him in my life at all?

I can't decide. I can't think at all anymore tonight.

So instead, I rush from his room and dive into my bed. Then I let the tears fall until the exhaustion pulls me into the first sleep I've had in days.

It's filled with nightmares, just like always.

CHAPTER TWENTY-SEVEN

EINAR

A furious storm has chased us below decks, throwing us off course.

It's beginning to feel like we'll never get off of this storms-damned ship. If I was superstitious, I would wonder if Ulla herself was responsible for the raging winds and the never-ending crashing of the waves.

The ship tilts to the left, and I nearly stumble into the wall.

My stomach was tenuous at best without the storm, but now it's much worse. A constant nausea twists my insides and my head throbs relentlessly. Though it's not quite time, I pull another bottle of the tonic from my pocket, downing it eagerly. Almost immediately, my stomach settles and my vision clears. The rest of the walk to the cabin isn't nearly so miserable.

Zaina sits on the edge of the bed, unbothered by the tilting of the ship as she idly traces Khijhana's metallic teeth. The chalyx sits placidly in front of her, also unaffected by the storm, or her mistress' examination.

Even seated, Khijha is nearly as tall as my wife. Chalyxes grow in direct proportion to their bond with their owner, and Zaina's recent brush with kidnapping has only made her beast more protective over her.

Which makes two of us.

I think of what I told Remy about life on the other side, wondering how much I believe we'll get there when Zaina is poised to offer herself up as a sacrificial lamb at every possible opportunity.

Her slim shoulders tense as though she senses my presence and the weight of the impending argument that accompanies it. But I don't want to fight with her about this again.

When Ulla took her from Palais Etienne, I forced myself not to fight because Zaina made it sound like she would fight to return to me. She admitted she hadn't, though. Not at first. For all her growth, Zaina will always be someone who will break herself for the people around her. The only way she will be out of danger is if we end this. Quickly.

With a sigh, I go to sit next to her, trailing my hand along her arm. She leans into my touch, though her stance tells me she's still on guard.

"Have you thought about life when this is all over?" I ask her in a low tone.

She freezes. "If this is your way of trying to make me feel guilty—"

"It isn't," I cut her off. "We both know that wouldn't work."

My tone is as neutral as I can manage, but she turns to

face me, peering up intently at me through her thick veil of lashes.

"You know that I love you," she says earnestly. The tumultuous waves rock the boat, making the gold flecks in her eyes shine in the cabin's rolling flicker of lantern light.

I nod. "I just wish that you could love yourself half as much."

She shakes her head softly. "It isn't about that. Don't you understand that if something happened to you, I wouldn't survive it? I wouldn't want to survive it, Einar."

I wrap my arm around her shoulders, pressing my lips against her forehead. Though I know Zaina loves me, she rarely says it explicitly, and it tugs at something inside of me to hear that she doesn't want to survive in a world where I don't.

Even if I feel the exact same way.

Even if I still wake up every night terrified of the same thing, that Ulla will find a way to take her from me.

"You asked me if I've thought about my life when this is over?" she says softly. "No. I haven't. I can't. I won't until we get through this because the second I allow myself to hope, to hold onto something in this life, Madame finds a way to rip it away from me."

"We can't go into this believing we won't come back out, Zaina," I murmur against her skin. "I have faith in you, and in us."

She lets out a harsh breath.

"Do you?" She backs up to look at me once more. "Because we still don't know what she will have turned me into by the time this is all over. Have you thought about *that*?"

I don't ask what she's referring to. I saw the moment she decided not to intervene with Katriane. I heard her say she would have happily used the dragons if not for the time it would have taken to subdue them.

I know who she is, and it doesn't scare me.

"I don't know what any of us will have to do to end this," I tell her. "But never doubt that I will still be standing here on the other side."

She holds my gaze, her eyes boring into mine. I see the moment she accepts my words, in spite of herself. Her shoulders relax ever so slightly, her features softening incrementally.

"Someday, I would like to find my family," she says quietly. "My first family."

The corner of my mouth tilts up. It's a small thing, for most people, but progress for my stubborn wife.

"Done," I say simply.

"Just like that?"

"I am a king, after all." I inject my tone with extra smugness to make her smile.

It works. She gives me a wan smirk.

"Are you?" she teases. "You haven't mentioned it before."

Zaina leans up then, her lips brushing against mine. She has gotten more comfortable with initiating affection in the time I've known her, but each kiss still feels like a victory. She is trusting me with the most vulnerable part of herself, and I will never take that for granted.

I tug her tighter against me, savoring the taste of her

lips and the feel of her body melting against mine. She pushes me back on the bed, straddling my hips, her lips never breaking contact.

My hands go to the bottom of her gauzy tunic, breaking the kiss just long enough to slip it up over her head. I trail my lips down her jaw, her collarbone, and lower, exploring every inch of exposed skin. She lets out a breathy sound, arching into me.

I could drown in that sound, consume it, live off of it for the rest of my life and die happy with her perfect skin against my lips.

I shift her until she's lying on her back and I'm balanced over her, sliding her sheer pants down her legs. Then she is bare before me, staring up with her swollen lips and her flushed cheeks.

Zaina tugs on my tunic until I pull it over my head in a single fluid motion. She devours me with her gaze, her eyes trailing down my chest, lingering on the V just above my waistline.

Then she reaches out to pull me against her, leaning up to place a kiss on my lips that is almost more tender than it is hungry.

"I love you," she whispers against my mouth.

This. This is what we're fighting for.

"I love you, too," I murmur back.

Then it's only me and my wife and a space away from the rest of this ship and the rest of the world and everything Ulla has tried to take from us.

But, of course, that can't last.

We have barely drifted off to sleep when we are awakened by the sound of the ship's alarm bells.

CHAPTER TWENTY-EIGHT

MELODI

The silence that stretches between Ari and me is almost painful in its precision. The world continues around me with more lessons from my aunt and cryptic conversations with the king, but I don't get so much as a vague impression from Ari.

The aching doesn't go away, though.

He asked me to trust him, and I'm trying. For that matter, I have no choice.

A gong sounds from across the room, the sound reverberating through the water in a low, ominous pulse that pulls me from my thoughts. I snap my attention up from the food I've been halfheartedly pushing around my plate.

Next to me, the king sits back in his chair, a wide grin stretching his lips upward as he shoves his own plate away. I can practically feel Ari tensing behind me, but I don't turn to look. And I don't open my mind to him, either.

Still, I brace myself. I know whatever is coming isn't going to be good.

"I have a treat for you tonight, Melodi." Cepheus' words rake over me with the finesse of a rusted blade, and I force myself to smile.

"Thank you, Grandfather," I say, before slurping down another oyster at his pointed glance.

I'm not really hungry, and the mollusk curdles on my tongue as men in chains are led into the dining room. Dark circles line their eyes, matching the scattered bruises on their bodies.

Some are missing limbs. Others are missing an eye or ear. One man is missing his nose. And yet, no one in this room seems to care. At least, not that they let on. Instead, they all cheer and excitedly raise their fists toward the king, bloodlust filling their eyes.

I wash down the rising bile in my throat with the liquid beads from my goblet, consuming every last one. Tonight's flavor reminds me of rye whiskey. I hope the effect is the same.

Once Cepheus rises from his chair to signal that dinner is over, we file from the room and out into an arena at the back of the palace. Hundreds of seats form a ring around a trench that dips low into the seabed.

Two thrones are erected at the front of the U-shaped space, separated from the rest of the crowd on a raised dais and walls on three sides. This is where my grandfather leads me. Danica and two of his favored commanders, along with Ari, are allowed in our box, as well, though they are forced to stand around us.

My stomach churns as the chained men are led to the center of the ring.

Voices ring out from the crowd, some calling for the

hand, some for the rack, and others for the dragon. My mind races, visions of the giant statue coming to the forefront of my thoughts.

I must not have my shields in place because whatever the king sees on my face has him grinning like a hungry shark. Finally, he raises his hands, quieting the crowd before fixing the full weight of his attention on me.

"What do you say, Granddaughter? Since these are the first games since your arrival, you decide."

My heart thrums violently in my chest, and I swallow down the rising panic threatening to take hold of me. I have been forced to witness torture before, more times than I care to recall, but I have never had to play an active role in someone else's suffering.

I don't want to do this. I can't.

"Peace, Kala." Ari's voice is a feather light touch in my mind, somehow closer than it should be, as if he is at my side, whispering the words so that only I can hear.

I check my shields, but they seem to be in order.

"No one else can hear me," he says. "Don't turn, and don't react."

I quickly rearrange my features into nonchalance, but not fast enough. My grandfather tilts his head curiously, and I force another false smile.

"Allow me a moment to consider," I say evenly, and he arches an eyebrow.

"Good." Ari's reassurance is a balm. "There are no good choices here, but the dragon will be faster."

He doesn't say that my grandfather will choose the worst one if I don't choose at all, and he doesn't remind me of the consequences of showing weakness here. We both know those things already.

So, I tuck away my trembling fingers and give my answer.

"The dragon," I say.

Cepheus' smile widens enough to show his glistening white teeth. He's more pleased by my decision than I would have expected, and it sends a shiver of terror down my spine.

"Tell them, Melodi. Give them the order," he says, gesturing toward the center of the podium. "Project that lovely voice of yours, and tell these prisoners their fate."

Ah, so that's why he looks pleased. I didn't balk, and now he has a chance to show off my savagery. It is a test— one I cannot fail. I move from the throne to the railing. I'm grateful for the water around me because if I had to walk right now, I'm certain my legs would not hold my weight.

Centering myself, I direct my thoughts outward, channeling them to the crowd as loudly as I can.

"The dragon," I declare, and the crowd erupts as I return to my seat.

Two of the prisoners are selected and freed from their chains, while the others are driven to the sidelines by the tips of the warriors' tridents. The ground shakes and the sea shivers as a large portcullis opens below the stands.

I had half-hoped the dragon was a nickname for a weapon, some quick way to put these poor souls out of their misery.

But a growl ripples through the sea, shaking the throne beneath me. It is the most harrowing noise I have ever heard. Another growl bellows out, and my body goes weak. Fear radiates off of the prisoners as they are forced to stand their ground in the center of the arena.

A ring of bubbles glides out of the doors, followed by the spark of orange flames and the hiss of fire meeting water. And then, I see it. With green and blue scales, yellow eyes and monstrously sharp teeth—the enormous head of the dragon.

It is somehow both beautiful and terrifying all at the same time and I can't bring myself to look away. My lips part in horror, my knuckles going white around the arms of the throne.

"Do not worry, Granddaughter. She will not hurt us," my grandfather says with a cruel smirk.

I think back to the book in my rooms and the few things I remember reading about its loyalty to the monarchy. It shouldn't be surprising that my grandfather has twisted that relationship the same way he does everything else in his orbit.

Flames shoot out from her mouth in a bright burst of color as she looks at the sacrifices we have given her. Black smoke is trapped in large bubbles, racing to the surface of the water as if they are trying to escape. There is an oily sheen coating them, almost iridescent as they spin and twist upward.

The dragon tilts her head—her yellow eyes flicking up to the box and fixing on me.

Something passes between us, some understanding or energy, and I know, in my soul, that my grandfather is right. Something snaps into place, as if she is acknowledging me as belonging to her.

Flashes of silver pull her attention back to the arena. The warriors are hurling rusted spears from the sidelines for the prisoners to attempt to defend themselves.

One of them lands in the prisoner's leg, and the crowd laughs uproariously. The dragon eats him first, her giant body ambling through the water before she devours him whole. The sound of crunching bone echoes through the arena, and the crowd cheers.

It's surreal, being in the midst of the gathering's macabre, fickle energy. Feeling their satisfaction as a man loses his life to the whims of a madman and his captive beast.

The dragon is barely finished spitting out the spear when she turns to lunge for the second man. Another growl rips through the water, the soundwaves blowing back my hair as she races after the prisoner.

I wonder if the man was a warrior before he was imprisoned. He's able to fight longer, to dive and swim and leap away from several blows that should have killed him. My chest tightens, hope almost rearing her naive head until one of the warriors on guard interferes.

She spears the prisoner with her silver trident when he swims too close to the line of warriors, and his weapon falls from his hands. Blood pools from his body like an angry geyser. Before he can so much as widen his eyes in shock, the dragon has devoured him too.

There is nothing but resignation on the faces of the other prisoners as two more are called to fight. Not horror, not repulsion, but acceptance. I would wonder why they bother to fight at all, but I already know the answer to that. A quick glance at my grandfather and the crowd tells me all I need to know.

It's for the show.

Violence is a sport here, and I have no doubt that their fates would be worse if they didn't acquiesce and give one final performance for their king.

For the next two hours the crunching of bones, the cries of the dying, and the cheers from the sadistic crowd echo through the arena on an endless, blood-curdling loop.

CHAPTER TWENTY-NINE

AIKA

*R*ain pours down, and lightning splits the sky in the distance. The storm is intense, but it isn't as menacing as the man standing before me on the deck.

Or Mayima, rather.

If I thought Einar was oversized for a human, it's nothing compared to the newcomer. Navy eyes glare at us from underneath a hood made of scales as his full lips curl back in what is obviously disdain.

Celestial hells.

For all of the Mayima who have been following us since we left Bondé, none have boarded our ship until now.

I draw my metal stars—not because I think they'll do any good, but because I'll be damned if I'm taken out without at least having a weapon in my hand. Remy stands beside me, slightly in front but not enough to interfere with my range of motion. His hand goes to his sword hilt, but he doesn't draw it.

The alarm bells finally quiet as the crew lines up in formation on either side of us, weapons at the ready while they await orders from their king. The Mayima looks both unconcerned and unimpressed. He opens his mouth, but my sister and Einar burst onto the deck before he can speak.

Zaina assesses the situation with a single sweep of her eyes. She doesn't go for her weapon, though. The Mayima turns to give her the same look he's giving the rest of us, but stops in his tracks when Khijhana rears forward. She stalks between him and my sister, her lips pulled back to reveal those stars-blessed silver teeth of hers.

He doesn't look nearly as blasé now.

"Peace, cat-dragon," he says, raising his hands. "If I had come to kill them, I would have by now."

Khijhana stops like she understood him, tilting her head to the side as she studies him from head to toe. Still, she doesn't move from where she is firmly planted in front of Zaina.

"I don't know about you, but usually, I don't just board someone's boat without an invitation unless my intentions are questionable," I call out over the booming of thunder and the rush of wind. "So, if you aren't here to kill us, then why are you here?"

A thought strikes me then just as lighting does the water. "Did Natia send you?"

He narrows his eyes at the name, his lips curling back in a snarl. "Natia is in no position to send anyone anywhere."

He might be talking about her social standing, but somehow I doubt it. Recalling her fear at helping us, a stab of guilt goes through me. Before I can voice my concern aloud, Remy cuts in.

"Then why are you here?"

"Kala—Melodi sent me."

I hardly have space to register the strange name he called her first because I'm too busy reeling from his flippant words. What the hell does he know about Melodi?

Khijhana growls, and he backs away. I'm not surprised to see Zaina step forward with fire in her eyes.

"What do you know about my sister?" she asks the question before I can.

He shrugs a shoulder.

"That she's more trouble than she's worth, at the moment," he mutters, looking irritably between Zaina and her enormous cat.

When Khijhana stalks toward him once again, he relents.

"Your *sister*—who is clearly not blood related to you, seeing as she's currently inhabiting the Palace of Mayim and you would be very much dead in her place—sent me to deliver the message that she is safe. Though, if I may add my own commentary, that's not strictly true, not that there's anything you can do about it from up here."

Another flash of lightning and the crash of thunder punctuates his words. Before any of us can respond, he continues.

"Of course, no one is strictly safe in Mayim, myself included if anyone spots me on this boat. So I'll be off now. Consider your message delivered, and I was never here."

He gives us a small salute and turns toward the side of the boat.

"Wait!" I call, rain pouring into my eyes and mouth as I dart forward. "You have to give us more than that."

His shoulders sag and he sighs loudly, but doesn't dive into the water. Instead, he spins on his heel to face us again, even though he clearly isn't happy about it.

"Even if I wanted to stay to chat with a bunch of humans—and whatever he is," he gestures in Einar's direction, casting him a suspicious look, "I have about a minute left before I need to get back into the sea. So ask your questions quickly."

"You called her Kala," Zaina rushes to say.

"It means—"

"Princess," she snaps impatiently. "Yes, I know."

Of course she does.

He blinks at her irritably, his lips parting before I cut him off with a question. "Her father is the king?"

"No," the Mayima corrects. "Her mother's father."

My mouth opens and closes as I process that. What it means for Mel. For Madame.

"Do you have a message for her?" he asks as another wave crashes onto the ship, sending a fresh surge of water sailing over the side, soaking us even more than we are now.

"Tell her we're going to the island—" Zaina says.

"Are we?" I cut her off. "If she's not in danger..."

"Then the rest of the world still is," Remy bites out. "Fundamentally, this changes nothing except that we have less collateral damage to worry about."

"One less player on the board," Einar agrees.

"But we have more time to plan now," I protest.

Usually, I'm happy to go in blind, but last time we tried to beat Madame with a half-arsed plan, people died. *Katriane* died.

"And put our entire lives on hold while Madame rebuilds her seat of power?" Zaina demands. "You were the one who said we needed to end this, and you weren't wrong."

"When Mel was in immediate danger," I argue.

It was different when there was urgency, but now...

"Tick tock, tiny human," the obnoxious Mayima says to me.

Looking from Remy's vaguely accusatory face to Zaina's determined one, I realize there isn't a choice here.

There never really was.

"Two weeks," I say. "That's how long before we land at Delphine."

He nods, turning to go, but Zaina's voice follows him.

"I have another message." He looks at her impatiently, but she stares him down. "You said there was nothing we could do if she was in danger, but that's not true. We have the dragons."

The Mayima's face pales.

"And if your king, or anyone, harms a single hair on my sister's head, we will not hesitate to use them." Zaina's tone is frigid in a way I've rarely heard it, eerily reminiscent of Madame's.

Even I can't tell if she's bluffing. She said herself that it was too late to go back for them. Besides that, we have no idea how the dragons would pose a threat to the Mayima all the way under the sea, so I would normally suspect she is posturing. But Zaina is not entirely reasonable when someone she loves is in danger.

Looking at her now, it isn't hard to believe she means every word.

CHAPTER THIRTY

MELODI

*A*ri follows me into my room when the contemptible show is over, shutting the door behind him.

There's a strange energy humming in my veins, an entirely different kind of tension since I all but ordered the deaths I had to watch today.

Logically, I know that isn't entirely true. But over and over, I hear myself think the word *dragon*. And over and over, I see them die by her fearsome teeth or claws or fire.

Then there is something else, something that stings as it dances along the edge of my rapidly fraying nerves.

Ari helped me tonight. I should be grateful for that—and I am, but he was inside my mind, despite my shields, something he didn't tell me he was capable of. He heard my thoughts when I was blocking him, not because of my own inadequacies, but because of yet another secret he has kept.

I think of all the times I thought my walls were up,

only to have him comment on my thoughts anyway. Or my emotions, as he does now.

"You're angry, Kala." His voice sounds in my head, but it's on the surface this time, instead of resounding deeply the way it did at the arena.

I think about his words. I don't get angry. Ever.

After a lifetime of watching my mother disappear into her own rage, seeing the destruction she wrought with it, it's not an emotion I usually allow myself.

But I can't deny something rising within me.

"I'm..." I trail off, the emotion dissipating as quickly as it came. In its place is a bone-deep weariness. I wrestle the tiara out from my curls and set it lightly on my night-stand. Napo eyes it with interest from where he was waiting on my bed.

Turning back to Ari, I finally finish my sentence. "I'm tired."

Nothing has ever felt truer.

I am tired of being surrounded by death and blood-shed and tyrants. Tired of Ari asking me to trust him, then keeping something new from me every time I turn around.

"I couldn't tell you," he gently responds to my thoughts.

I shake my head. "Stay out of my head unless you're prepared to invite me into yours."

He sighs, watching Napo wind his tentacle through my tiara. "Would do that if I could, Kala, but it isn't that simple."

Would do that if he could invite me into his head? Or stay out of mine?

"The things I know are dangerous," he answers my unasked questions.

"Of course they are." Bitterness soaks my tone, potent and unfamiliar.

Remorse emanates from him in waves, but it's not as strong as his determination. He must have lowered his shields enough to let me sense that, I realize, but not enough for me to hear his inner thoughts the way he has clearly been able to hear mine.

"Is this the same reason why I can sense your emotions?" I ask.

He hesitates, and another wave of bitterness hits me, powerful enough to make him wince.

"Someone will hear—"

"Did you know all along that we could communicate this way?" I interrupt him. "You've just been listening and feeling everything I feel?"

"I made no secret that I could hear you. I believe I've told you multiple times to work on your seas-damned shields." Another of his hedging answers.

"That's not what I mean, and you know it."

His sea-green gaze meets mine, his chest rising and falling, the muscle in his jaw twitching as he contemplates his answer.

"Yes, I knew."

"And even though you knew it was a violation, even though you must have known that I already felt violated —" I cut off, shoving away thoughts of Damian's too-warm hands on my skin.

Not that it matters. Ari has apparently heard them all by now.

OF SONGS AND SILENCE

His gaze darkens. "I am nothing like—"

"No," I say quickly. "You aren't. But this…" I gesture between us, not able to articulate the way this hurts unexpectedly.

"I did what I had to do to keep you—"

"Don't you dare say *safe*," I hiss. "Don't talk about protecting me when this, not knowing, is driving me insane. You won't tell me why we can communicate this way."

Silence is my only answer, along with a tightening of his shields.

"Just like you won't tell me why I see your face in my dreams," I push.

"Kala." He says the word like a warning, like he has so many times before, but this time, I ignore it.

"Just like you won't tell me why I feel like I can't breathe when you're not around. Why I crawl out of my skin if you stray too far from me." Somehow throughout this conversation I have moved closer to him, his face just inches from mine. "Why even now, even when I deserve to be upset, every part of your body calls to mine, and you're the only stars-blasted thing I can see, and—"

"Did it ever occur to you that you are not the one who couldn't handle the truth of this?" he barks, closing what little distance is between us, his lips brushing my forehead. His touch is a gentle contrast to his impassioned tone. "The consequences of it? Don't you understand that I—"

Whatever he was about to say is abruptly cut off by the groan of the door. Danica stands in the doorway, her features pinched with admonishment and something strangely close to grief.

But not a hint of surprise.

CHAPTER THIRTY-ONE

MELODI

*A*ri stands frozen for three solid heartbeats before he slowly stretches to his full height. His features are colder than I've ever seen them, masking the panic I feel building in him despite his shields.

"Commander Ariihau," my aunt says. "You may resume your duties in the hallway."

"Yes, Kala'ni Danica." He hesitates ever so slightly, and she gives a prolonged blink.

"I trust you're finished helping Kala with her shield training," Danica says, her features devoid of the lie we all know she is telling.

Ari's shoulders relax, incrementally.

"Yes, Kala'ni Danica," he says again, turning to leave with markedly less hesitation than before.

Once the door shuts behind him, my aunt gives me a long, lingering look. I'm not sure I'll ever get used to the resemblance between her and Mother, not just her beautiful umber skin, violet hair and full lips.

It's in the way Danica moves. The tilt of her wrist as she holds her glass. The way she meticulously and subtly checks each food dish for poison. The way she narrows her eyes and sees so much more than I mean for her to, like she does right now.

I'm not sure if she intends it to be intimidating with the twin of the expression I had been raised with back home, but Mother's intimidation is more than a carefully cultivated selection of responses and reactions.

It is based on her volatility, her cruelty, two things that Danica lacks. So I wait patiently for my aunt to make her point.

"What you're doing is dangerous." Her tone is clipped.

"So I've been told." Over and over again by a man who refuses to say anything more on the subject.

"Stupid girl," she bites out with more vigor than I expect. "You may have been told, but you haven't begun to understand."

"How could I? When no one will begin to explain." I'm less demanding than pleading at this point.

Her expression softens, though the warning doesn't leave it. "Even explanations here are dangerous."

I meet her eyes solidly. "So is ignorance."

She levels me with another scrutinizing glance.

"You are so like him," she finally says.

The blood drains from my face. "The king?"

"Your father."

I go still, holding whatever version of breath I have underwater. This is the first time she has consented to speak about him, and I don't want to startle her out of it.

She shakes her head again, like she's come to some sort of conclusion. Finally, she sits down on the small sofa in my room, gesturing for me to join her.

"Makani was a villager," she states.

"But that's—"

"Forbidden, yes."

From the haunted look in her eyes, I'm not so sure I want to hear this story anymore.

"He was…earnest. Straightforward. Kind. He was a musician. That's how they met."

"Because of his music?" I ask.

She nods solemnly. "He was playing. She was dancing, in one of the villages."

I would suspect her of lying if I didn't feel the truth of her statement. My mother, dancing. I can't picture it, can't even fathom it. She never even stayed for music lessons at the house, and wouldn't allow my sisters to play freely. If there was music, it had to be for a purpose, to prepare for some social event. Even then, she got no enjoyment out of it. At least, not that I could see.

With something close to a sigh, my aunt closes her eyes. The next thing I know, images are flitting through my mind.

It's my mother.

I know because even then, she had a more calculating gleam to her eye than my aunt does. Still, she is almost unrecognizable with a soft smile on her face as she shoves her curls out of her face and moves around with abandon.

Behind her, a man watches with unabashed awe in his pale green eyes. His skin is several shades lighter than mine, but his lips pull up into the same full smile I see in the mirror, and his short-cropped hair is the exact shade of crimson as my own.

When the song is over, he goes to her, stretching out a hand and placing a wrapped bundle in her palm.

She unwraps the package, dropping the seaweed to the ground. Her eyes widen in something like wonder as she stares at an iridescent conch shell on a delicate chain. My hands automatically go to the necklace I haven't taken off since she gave it to me years ago.

She wraps her arms around his neck, pressing a kiss to his lips in a movement more genuine and gentle than I have ever known her capable of.

The image fades, and my aunt opens her eyes.

In all the times I've wondered who my father was, it never truly occurred to me that Mother might have loved him. That she grieved him. It doesn't undo her sins. It doesn't even come close.

I picture her in my room, her hands in my hair—the red spiral curls that are identical to his. *You are entirely his.*

Not Damian's. My father's. The man she loved. The man she *lost.*

Did he change his mind about the danger? Did she leave before he could be punished? Is he out there somewhere, unaware that he has a daughter?

My aunt gives a small shake of her head. Once again, I have allowed myself to be naive. To be hopeful in a world that doesn't allow for such fanciful notions. Tears stab at the back of my eyes, and she gives me a knowing look.

"He was right not to tell you. You are too free with your thoughts by half."

Before I can be bothered by her cryptic words, she places a slim hand on my shoulder. "It's time to work on your shields."

CHAPTER THIRTY-TWO

ARIIHAU

*O*nce I'm sure she's safe with Kala'ni, I take advantage of the privacy to sneak out of the palace. I was too reckless, too free with our conversation. If anyone else overheard us, I would be dead.

And her punishment would be far worse than that. Guilt snakes through me once again, but I remind myself that I couldn't have told her sooner. Even now, I don't know how much Danica will reveal. If she'll tell her the truth I've been fighting so hard not to.

Before I leave the palace grounds, I grab one of the newer recruits from the barracks and send her up to keep an extra set of eyes on Kala's door. Though Napo would happily take the job, he's not as strong as the warriors are, even if he thinks otherwise.

Since Kane isn't here, I'm left with Noa—one of the rare decent souls amongst the latest Warrior class. She's also extremely skilled, working her way up nearly as quickly as I did at her age.

More importantly, since I trained her, she's loyal to *me*. Not the king. Not the rebels.

Just as I expected, she eagerly takes off to follow my orders. I wouldn't leave at all, but it's been too long since I've checked in with the others. After what happened with Jopali's attack on the way here, I know I can't wait any longer.

I'm just outside the palace gates when a familiar voice greets me.

"It's about time," Kane's sardonic tone calls.

Relief crashes over me. He's safe, and I'll have him with me to face this meeting with the rebels.

"How did your visit with your parents go?" I ask casually, looking around to see if anyone is nearby.

"As well as could be expected," he responds. "Didn't realize they had a newfound interest in travel."

Ah. So Kala's family was on the seas, after all.

"Incidentally," he adds in an undertone. "Did you know Kala is actually the nicest member of her family? And potentially the only sane one."

From the glimpses I've gotten of her thoughts, I did, in fact, know that.

"I thought she was devious and underhanded," I say sarcastically as we catch an undercurrent to the reef's edge.

He rolls his eyes. "You can't blame me for wondering if she might be a master at faking her thoughts. The king certainly is. But no one can pretend that well."

I hear what he doesn't say, also. Kala has a warmth, a humanity, that can't be manufactured. Thinking about her just exacerbates the itchy, uncomfortable feeling I get with each mile I put between us.

Kane doesn't comment on her anymore, and I try to distance my thoughts as much as I can as we wind our way to the hidden cavern. Lantern fish offer a subtle glow, guiding us all the way down to the seafloor.

The water here is colder and darker, making it nearly impossible to see more than a few feet in front of us. Still, we know exactly where we're going—the low hum of angry voices guides us to one of the far rooms where Lani and her men are already waiting.

I brace myself, already preparing for the inevitable argument. Sure enough, the atmosphere is just as icy as the deep waters of the cave.

"Take a break from cozying up to Kala and murdering your own to grace us with your presence, Commander?" Lani, the de facto leader of the rebellion, spits the words out with unveiled venom.

Kane stiffens at my back, his posture defensive, but I gesture for calm. We could fight our way out of this room if we needed to, but at what cost? We need this rebellion, now more than ever. And they need us, if they stand half a chance at overthrowing the king.

"You're the one who wanted him in a coveted position, Lani," Kane's tone is even, but it's edged with pure steel. "Don't think to punish him for doing what he had to in order to keep it."

Her red eyes practically glow with anger, but she considers my cousin's words.

"It's true that he's close enough to the girl to take care of the spawn," someone suggests.

It takes everything in me not to snarl at the person who insulted Kala and suggested I murder her in one go.

Even if that had been the plan, *before*.

Before I found her.

Before I knew who she was to me.

Before I knew who she was. Period.

Kane puts a steadying hand on my shoulder while we both ride out the wave of suggestions and accusations.

"But we need him on the king," another warrior counters. "He's the only one strong enough to have a chance, even with a blunt force attack."

"And we're just going to trust him?" one of the villagers demands. "After what he did to Jopali's crew?"

Finally, I speak up. "Jopali received no fate he did not bring upon himself. I told him not to attack. I warned him what would happen, but he wouldn't listen."

I had been given less than a minute to make the decision of whether to hurt my own people or let them hurt Kala. It hadn't been a choice at all. I will add their names to the list of people I have killed, that I *will* kill to keep her safe.

Everyone in this room knows that I have only achieved my rank because of the hard decisions I've had to make. It's something that Lani has always understood better than most. Insisted on it, even.

Which makes me wonder if Jopali was acting on her orders. Her eyes narrow when they meet mine, and I know she suspects something else is at play.

"That may well be," she bites out. "But you have yet to explain your position on the girl."

179

She's choosing her words carefully, having seen how I reacted to the subtle threat.

Clenching my jaw, I resolve to be more careful. I am not sure what I can tell them yet, but for now, I need to stall for time.

"I could hardly let myself be overtaken when the king knows I am capable," I explain. "We can't take on Cepheus yet, unless one of you has a plan to attack right when his guard is at its strongest?"

Silence greets me, but no one argues. Lani might technically be the leader here, but even the rebels are not immune to the rules of trial by combat. And I have never lost yet.

I just need to keep it that way.

CHAPTER THIRTY-THREE

MELODI

*M*y aunt stayed most of the night to help me work on my shields.

She taught me how to take certain thoughts and lock them away into a chest in the back of my mind where not even the king can reach them. She didn't say that, of course, but the implication was there.

She didn't say anything else about my father, either. Not that I asked.

It's a strange feeling, mourning someone I never knew. I wonder how my mother survived, and why she bothered to build an empire on land if she was grieving and trying to stay alive.

I add that to my growing list of questions, trying to tamp down the rampant anxiety I feel once my aunt leaves me alone. It continues late into the morning, like a thousand fire ants marching across my skin.

It's more than my questions, or even my fear. It's the same gnawing, empty feeling I get when Ari is too far away for too long.

Finally, I can't stand it anymore. I promised him I wouldn't open the door to his room again, but I can't seem to help myself. I knock once, twice, but there is no answer. Finally, I crack the door open, quietly calling his name—hoping if I can at least see him, talk to him, some of this frustrating feeling might abate. But he isn't here.

Napo stretches from where he's laying in the window, his dark eyes widening happily as he takes me in.

"Where is he?" I ask, and he shrugs an annoyed tentacle before swimming through the door into my room. Whether he's irritated with me, or Ari, I can't quite tell, but he's soon happily trying on one of my tiaras and ignoring me.

Closing the door behind him, I swim to the front door. Where Ari usually stands guard, there is instead a young woman with emerald braids and rose-colored eyes. She wears the outfit of all the Warriors, a sharply cut vest that shows off a deep V of cleavage. Her striking features are carved into a serious expression.

"Where's—the Commander?"

She dips her head sharply in a formal bow. "He didn't say, Kala. Only that he will return shortly. I will accept any punishment you feel is necessary for the disappointment."

My lips part in horror, though why I should be surprised at this point is beyond me.

"That's—" I start to say *ridiculous* before I realize I will be insulting the king. "There is no punishment," I tell her instead. "Please tell the Commander I wish to speak with him when he returns."

"Yes, Kala."

"Thank you..." I trail off until she supplies her name.

"Lieutenant Noa."

"Thank you, Lieutenant Noa."

My nervousness doesn't abate, though. The last place in the world I want to be is trapped in my room, trapped anywhere. Especially when I don't know where Ari is, or if he's all right, or if he's getting a new assignment—

"Is there something else I can do for you, Kala?" Noa asks, confusion in her tone.

It's interesting that Ari is so concerned with my safety all the time, but he has left one of the youngest soldiers I have yet seen to guard me. Her trident is bronze, something I have come to realize denotes a section of rank.

No sooner has the thought crossed my mind than a shadow falls over us, and Noa reaches for her trident, moving to stand in front of me with lightning fast reflexes. She may be young, but she is still a soldier, clearly very well trained. I don't need to see around her to know who it is. The feeling on my skin abates ever so slightly, even before I hear the familiar voice.

"At ease, Lieutenant Noa. I'll take over from here."

The Warrior places a fist over her chest to acknowledge the order, but her cheeks light up in a pretty blush, her eyes all but sparkling.

Something ugly twists inside of me, and I try to stamp it down before she can catch wind of my thoughts. But of course, I can't hide it from Ari. He looks from her to me, then back to her as though something is dawning on him.

It eases my mind slightly that he didn't seem aware of her obvious attraction.

She turns to bow her head to me, then takes off down

the hall with one last look in his direction. Ari gestures for me to go back to my room. Instead of staying to guard the door, he follows me in. I drink in the sight of him before I can stop myself.

My gaze rakes down his body, scanning him for injuries or any sign of where he's been. Belatedly, I realize I know nothing about his life here.

Does he have family nearby?

A random villager he is visiting because he has been all but chained to me for the last several weeks? Have I been so selfish and focused on whatever strange pull exists between us, that I haven't even stopped to consider his life before we met?

Does he have a girlfriend? A wife?

Bile rises in my throat, panic sending my pulse racing through my veins. A small twitch of his lips belies his amusement.

"Peace, Kala." The words resound deep in my mind. "There is no one. I had business with some other Warriors. I've never had time for any other...entanglements, nor interest in them."

Relief crashes over me in a wave, and his expression twists in a rare bit of mischief.

"And if I had been...visiting a random villager, I would have been gone a lot longer."

Heat surges through me, my body starting to tingle for an entirely different reason when a new voice interrupts us.

"My, how I haven't missed this," Kane intones. "Shields, Kala, for the love of the seas."

Now I see why Ari didn't close the door. I rapidly throw my walls into place, turning to inspect Kane. He, too, seems unharmed, thank the stars.

"Did you find them?" I ask.

"I did," he responds, shutting the door.

When I raise an eyebrow at him, he smirks.

"There might not be a blood relation, but you look just like the pretty, angry one when you do that."

"Zaina," I supply.

He nods. "She made some interesting threats. I couldn't quite tell if she meant them."

I can't help but grin at that. Aika is the one who bluffs. If Zaina made threats, she absolutely meant them.

"Can you show me?" I ask.

He looks at Ari, who reluctantly nods. I narrow my eyes in confusion. Can he not do it? Danica didn't make it seem like it was overly difficult, but then, she is more skilled with her mind than most Mayima I've encountered.

"It's considered…intimate," Kane explains. "And I don't fancy being run through by our dear Commander's trident today."

I glance from him to Ari, my heartbeat picking up speed.

Part of me wants to deny that it's his concern, but even if he weren't in charge of keeping me safe, I know perfectly well how I felt mere moments ago when I thought he was visiting someone else in the village.

So I keep my thoughts to myself.

There's a gentle prodding at my shields, and I slowly

take them down until an image comes into my mind. Unlike the fuzzy vision I got from my aunt, this one is clear, perhaps because it's so much more recent.

Longing shoots through me.

Aika is as fierce as ever, but I wonder if I imagine the tired lines on her skin. Still, she smirks, and the man at her side mirrors the expression. There's what looks to be a furry tail wrapped around her wrist, but whatever animal it belongs to is tucked out of sight in her sleeve.

Then comes Zaina, so beautiful it almost hurts to look at her. She stands behind a massive white…tiger? Cat-dragon, Kane calls it. A giant of a man guards her back, nearly the size of the Mayima.

I watch as my sisters argue—predictably—then as Zaina stares down a Mayima twice her size and threatens him with the very creature that nearly killed her—the dragons. Her features are carved into an icy determination, her eyes flooded with rage.

It would be terrifying, if it was directed at me rather than on my behalf.

As it stands, I never thought I would see the day where Aika was the more mild of the two. Then again, Aika hasn't lost a sister yet.

Stars, how I miss them both.

"Thank you," I say quietly when it's over.

Kane nods, excusing himself, but I barely hear him; all I can think about are my sister's faces. Their words. Their plan.

Ari doesn't leave my side, his concerned gaze searching my features. I want to reassure him, but I still can't wrap my head around what I've seen. They're going to Delphine.

And they're going to kill my mother.

CHAPTER THIRTY-FOUR

MELODI

*W*hen enough time passes that Ari is forced to retreat into the hallway, I still have not come to terms with the emotions running rampant through my mind.

Isn't this what I wanted? For someone to take Mother down? To stop her cruelty and sever the hold she has on us?

I remember the image of her, bright and happy and in love. It doesn't change anything, doesn't begin to undo the things that she has done. She needs to be stopped.

A knife twists in my gut all the same.

Is it for her? Or because I worry that whatever is left of my sisters' souls will go when she does?

When Moli comes to dress me for dinner, I don't have any answers.

She quietly drapes me in another outfit made of golden scales, shells, and jewels. A gilded crown rests on my head, and bracelets adorn my upper arms and wrists.

Moli is always competent, but she seems even more

determined to make me perfect tonight, taking time to twist each of my curls into submission and adorning me with make-up for a change.

She gently applies ink to my eyelids like the kohl we use on land, then crushes red flowers to paint my lips and stain my cheeks. Something niggles at the back of my mind as we go through the steps.

Tonight is different somehow. I am being plucked and painted for more than one of the usual court dinners.

Once I'm ready, I meet Ari in the hall. His expression shutters as he takes me in. Warmth pools low in my stomach and that invisible thread between us pulls taut.

Shaking the feeling away, I regain my senses and stuff the thoughts deep down in the recesses of my mind. He tenses and does the same, keeping his shields tight as he stoically leads me to the dining hall.

When we arrive, the doors are shut. Just before the guards open them, the chilling sound of a gong rings out, vibrating the water around us.

Every muscle in my body tenses as I consider the last time I heard that sound. The decision I was forced to make afterward. The lives that were lost.

Will Ari and I be next?

"Peace, Kala." His words wrap around me, holding me steady.

I allow them to calm my racing thoughts as the massive door swings open.

There is a pervasive feeling in the water, something like dread mingled with desire. It surges through the room, from table to table as they watch me pass. I don't look at them, though. I keep my gaze fixed on the king.

His usual haughty expression is present, and his violet eyes are full of violence.

Danica isn't far from him tonight, but she remains just as steadfast as usual, never once looking in my direction. I feel her prodding my shields though, in warning.

As usual, the rest of the room stays standing until every member of the royal family is seated. I keep my features neutral as the first course is served, waiting for the other shoe to drop—for whatever game my grandfather is playing to begin.

I don't have to wait long.

Before I can even reach for my fork, the king gains our attention with a wave of his hand.

"As I said earlier," he begins, and Ari tenses behind me. "I have a special announcement to make."

The room quiets and, once again, all eyes fall on me.

"Now that my granddaughter has been restored to me, I have finally decided to name my heir." He pauses for dramatic effect, allowing his words to sink in.

A thrum of anticipation takes over the room, mingled with shock. And, in Ari's case, horror. I fight not to turn around to take in his expression, but his dread fuels my own even before the king speaks again.

"I have decided to hold a competition for my granddaughter's hand," he proclaims. "To find the strongest among you, to become the next king."

Murmurs rise from those seated around the table.

My body grows hot and then cold. A shiver races up my spine and I fight down a stab of terror, of fury—emotions that compete and war for dominance.

The strongest will inherit.

This is what he meant before. Not me. Not a woman. But *this*.

I move my hands to my lap, pinching my thighs, digging my nails into my flesh in an effort to stop the trembling in my fingers. It shouldn't be any different than being promised to Damian. It shouldn't matter when I have never had a say in my future before. But that was before—

I stop myself before I think of his name, his face, the pull I have to him, or the visceral urge to run into his arms and make him take me far, far away from here.

"Those who wish to compete for their place at her side shall do so, to the death."

That final word ricochets through the room, echoing off the walls and back to every single eligible noble in the room. It isn't a surprise, not to them or to me. Everything here is death.

The king takes a full minute to revel in the impact of his proclamation before he delivers the final blow.

"The games begin at dawn."

CHAPTER THIRTY-FIVE

ZAINA

y mind has not quieted since the Mayima left.

The low hum of conversation drifts over from the card table as Remy and Aika try to distract themselves while I sit with Khijhana in the corner.

I idly trace her tooth for what has to be the thousandth time. Well, not idly. I wiggle it quite intentionally. Once I realized that she, like a growing human, would lose her teeth, I started to experiment. It's nearly as long as my finger, and at least twice as wide—the size of a small, discreet dagger.

There may be a necessary risk, and I may not be able to keep her from this fight, but I'll be damned if I don't at least try to protect the creature in this world that has been the most unselfishly loyal to me.

I have no pain relieving tonic strong enough to feel comfortable yanking the tooth out, so I gently work it back and forth as I have been doing since we left. Pumpkin watches with curiosity, no doubt wondering how to pocket the shiny, metallic treasure as soon as I've wiggled it out.

I shoo him away, and he retreats to my sister's neck, though he stops at the desk along the way to pilfer the ring from my distracted husband's hand. A smile tugs at my lips, in spite of my mood.

"Did you mean it?" Aika asks.

Her voice carries a little more than before and I know that the question is for me. I don't ask what she's referring to. The days on the sea have put us all on edge, and she is no exception.

"Yes," I say simply.

"I thought you were against going back for the dragons," she shoots back, mostly, I suspect, just because she's itching for a fight after the storm made it impossible for us to spar.

I sigh. I had been against using the dragons in general, except as a last resort. But I'll do what I have to, every time, to keep my family safe.

Still, Aika's words chafe.

"I was against burning people alive, too, until I did it to keep you from getting caught."

Despite the fact that she was the one who initiated this conversation, Aika's eyes tighten. With another sigh, I give her a somewhat apologetic look.

Einar looks up from where he studies a map of Delphine. "We can hope it won't come to that."

Even knowing him as I do, I can't be certain if his words are meant to support me or to stay my hand. Remy says nothing, but I feel his eyes on me all the same, his silent judgment of my selective morality.

"The Mayima might be brutal in general," Einar continues. "But being royalty will afford her a certain amount of protection, and the one who came was clearly somewhat affectionate toward her."

I had picked up on that as well. There was a certain begrudging protectiveness, at the very least, and the fact that he was deigning to deliver her message at all spoke volumes.

I nod, having no other response Einar wants to hear right now.

Picturing the great silver-white beast that saved me from Damian's clutches, I *do* hope things won't come to that. But if they do, I know I will do what needs to be done.

The resignation on his face tells me he knows that, too.

EINAR AND REMY have taken to having a drink on the deck every night. Usually, I use this time to spar with Aika, but we're going into battle soon, and we cannot go in divided.

So tonight, I go to Remy.

Einar reads me as well as he always does, excusing himself when I make my presence known. Remy doesn't look away from where he's staring at the reflection of stars on the churning, black sea.

At least, I assume that's what he's doing. His chestnut colored waves obscure his features from me. I step into my husband's place, helping myself to some of the whiskey they were drinking.

The minutes tick by in a silence Remy doesn't bother to break. I don't either. Now that I'm here, I'm not quite sure what to say.

Do I apologize for a choice I would make again? *Would I do it again?*

I take another sip from the glass Einar left behind, already knowing the answer. In the same circumstances with the same information I had at the time, I would have made that choice every time.

But knowing what I know now, that it made no difference in the end…

Finally, I clear my throat.

"If I had known the way that things would go, I never would have hesitated," I say.

Remy takes a long swig of his drink, his gaze still fixed on the open sea. "Has anyone ever told you that you suck at apologies?"

I almost laugh. Almost.

"I don't actually apologize often enough for anyone to comment on it," I answer honestly.

"Now, that, I can believe." There's a hint of the teasing tone he used to make with everyone, though it's buried under something I can't quite name.

Another stilted beat of silence passes between us. I try not to think of his mother's eyes, the same shade of cinnamon as his. The sound of her neck snapping and the look of horror on Remy's face. He's likely battling the same memories.

"I am sorry for what happened," I say sincerely.

He turns to look at me, blowing out a sigh. "You can live with your guilt, Zaina, and I'll live with mine."

I hear everything he isn't saying. He doesn't blame me, not entirely. He doesn't hate me. But he won't offer me absolution, either.

Which is fair. He's right. We'll all have to live with our mistakes, but there's no sense forgetting where the real blame lies.

"I just want to end this." My voice is nearly as tired as I feel.

"So we can all move on with our lives?" he asks, the slightest hint of mocking to his tone.

"That, too." I meet his eyes solidly, giving him a truth in lieu of the apology he didn't want or need. "But honestly, at this point...I want her to pay for the things that she's done."

He levels me with an appraising look, clinking his glass against mine before downing the rest of his drink.

"So do I."

CHAPTER THIRTY-SIX

ARIIHAU

*E*motions war within me, but I work to keep them at bay, for Kala's sake.

"Peace, Kala." I infuse the words with all of the confidence I don't feel.

I knew Cepheus was planning something for her. I just didn't know it would be this soon. My mind races as I think of plans, contingencies, moving up the timeline for the rebels. Anything and everything to stop this from happening.

Relief thrums through me when Kala clears her expression, nodding. But alongside my relief, there is fury, too, because this has been her life. Playing games of obedience while she's promised to a man who knows nothing but brutality.

It occurs to me that I'm no different, just another in a long line of people who don't deserve her goodness. But that hardly matters now.

When I escort Kala back to her room, I follow her in under the pretense of checking for intruders. Once I'm sure we're out of sight, I cave to my never-ending desire to have her in my arms, needing to feel her and comfort her and give her just a small sign that she matters to me, even if she doesn't understand why that's so important to her.

Her body melds perfectly against mine. She lets out a sigh of relief as she wraps her arms around my waist, burying her face in my chest. All I want to do is keep her here, keep her safe.

Guilt stabs through me at all the things I'm forced to keep from her. This bond is difficult enough to adjust to, even understanding it, though I grew up with the lore. I know she thinks she's going crazy, that she doesn't understand the way she has become my entire world.

I can't explain that to her, not when her shields are still fickle, not when she would be the one who took the brunt of that punishment. But I can give her something.

"I promise you, he will not win, not this time." Though I am intentionally vague, lest anyone get a glimpse of this from her mind, I let her feel the truth in my words.

For a rare change, I let her feel the part of me that is inextricably tied to her, the part of me that could no sooner lie to her than I could cut off my own arm. It's the closest I can come to reassuring her, about her fate, and about ours.

She pulls back to look up at me through her lashes, surprise widening her eyes, and I know she hears everything I'm not saying about my loyalties, about how seriously I take protecting her.

For the first time since the day Kane pulled her into the ocean, her eyes spark with something close to hope.

AFTER KALA GOES TO BED, I call upon Lieutenant Noa to guard her door once more.

I'm not worried about the king trying to hurt her, not now that he's using her to distract his people and choose his successor, conveniently weeding out his enemies in the process.

Once Noa is in place and Kala is sleeping fitfully, I make my way back to the cavern where I know the rebels will be meeting in light of this news. Kane is already here, greeting me with a nod when I glide in.

Lani looks at me with her jaw clenched.

"We have to strike before the end of the tournament," she says, clearly bracing herself for an argument from me.

Which is fair, since normally I would remind her that we don't have time to plan this, don't yet have the numbers. But I will die before I let Kala pay the price for our hesitation. Before I let someone put their hands on her against her will.

"I couldn't agree more," I respond to Lani's obvious surprise. "But we will be keeping Kala alive."

My voice is pure steel, leaving no room for disagreement. Instead of a clamoring of protest, the silence of several shields locking into place is the only response I get. Lani looks at me with her too-knowing gaze for a stilted moment before tilting her head toward one of the far rooms of the cavern. I nod at Kane and he returns it, an agreement to watch my back.

A lantern fish swims in with us, offering a flicker of

light in the otherwise complete darkness of the cave. Kane slides a heavy rock into place to act as a door to give us a modicum of privacy. Though I can hear Kala through the walls, that is a side effect of our bond. No one here should be able to discern our conversation from this distance, with a barrier between us.

Once the rock is in place, I lock eyes with Lani.

"We can't leave her alive," she says, more cautious than usual.

She knows, as I do, how easily I could best her in a fight. How serious I am about this. But I don't want to take out the leader of the rebellion unless she poses an actual threat to Kala, not when I respect her as a person and this might be our only real option.

"Yes," I counter. "We can."

Lani lets out an irritable snort. "This is not just because I hate that family, although I do. I am happy to leave Danica alive since she poses no threat to anyone, but do you honestly think Melodi wants to live a life where she's fought over and claimed by every warrior who wants their chance on the throne? Even if we tried to exile her..."

"What if we controlled who she married?" The question hangs in the water between us, and Lani's eyes narrow. "It would be an easier transition for the people anyway. No threat of the king, but no instability of arguing over who is on the throne."

"You want to claim Kala for yourself?" She sounds less offended than curious.

Closing my shields, I nod. "You wanted me to be king."

"And you refused, forcefully and at great length." She

crosses her arms, the manta ray tattoo on her bicep rippling with the motion.

"Things have changed," I say flatly.

"You would force her to take your hand?" This time, there is no real curiosity.

She asks like she already knows the answer. I could lie, or I could hedge. But she suspects already, and I need her on my side. So I give her the truth, saying the words for the first time since Kala's face appeared in my dreams, since her song reverberated in my being.

"I won't have to. Kala is my soulmate."

CHAPTER THIRTY-SEVEN

MELODI

The day of the first competition arrives, and all I want to do is disappear. I don't want to witness the brutality that's coming, even if the contenders signed up for this. They flock into the arena like their deaths aren't imminent, treating their fates like the game my grandfather has turned them into.

Are they fighting for power? For status? For a chance to make a change?

Or do they just want to own me?

I'm not sure it matters when their hands will be stained with the blood of their friends.

Once again, I find myself forced to sit in the royal box, staring down into an arena, waiting for the bloodshed to begin and wondering how the people rationalize it all. With my shields fully in place, I remind myself of Ari's words.

This will not stand.

I don't know how he plans on making sure of that, but I felt the truth of his words, the strength of his determination. Despite the reality we find ourselves in, the constant, lurking danger, I do trust him—not to tell me things, but to keep me safe.

That helps me bolster myself against whatever happens next. So, I fight the rising panic, locking it away in that chest in the back of my mind. I don't think about which of the contenders will win.

Because it doesn't matter. It can't.

Instead, I work on my shields. I imagine the strongest steel surrounding every emotion, every thought. I lock them away, too, and stare blankly ahead.

A satisfied smirk rests on the king's lips as he looks from me to the crowd and I fortify my walls even more. He stands to address the arena, and more specifically the forty-seven Mayiman nobles who proudly await their chance to die.

"Today, you fight for your future," he announces. "For the privilege of joining my family."

The crowd cheers. I study each competitor, memorizing their faces, each shade of their hair, the vivid color of their eyes that I can make out even from all the way up here.

They may not be part of the Warrior class, but there is no mistaking their strength. I can't imagine they would have entered this contest otherwise, not when their lives are on the line.

One man stands out to me in particular. His fair skin nearly blends with the pale silver strands of his hair. While the others are watching the king, his lime green gaze is locked onto me. He doesn't leer, though, not like the others have.

There is something in his expression that I can't quite read as he subtly dips his head toward me before looking away again. I carefully lock the exchange away, trying not to read into it as the first four names are announced.

"Koa Ione, Akamu Hale, Rangi Palakiko, Hohepa Lai," Cepheus calls and the men step forward.

They are immediately fitted with scaled armor and helmets, each of them given a short sword and a trident while the rest are led to the sidelines.

A gong signals for them to begin and the Mayima cut through the water like marlins. Sword meets sword. Trident meets flesh. The cries of battle and pain resound in my head as blood is shed and bones are crushed.

The first to die is the youngest of the four—Rangi. His orange hair falls over his face like flames as his lifeless body floats above the other fighters. The sharks are already circling, called by the scent of first blood, waiting for their next meal to be delivered.

They thrash, and bite and tear skin from bone, and soon there is nothing left but the faint memory of the heir to House Palakiko.

I wonder if his family will mourn him. Or if they only feel the pang of failure.

The weight of my grandfather's stare pulls my attention back to the battle below. Does he care who wins? Does he care what happens to me? Or to the future of his kingdom?

Is this little more than another test? A game? I tuck the questions away, carefully emptying my mind once again as I watch the next two men meet their deaths.

By the time we leave the arena, a dozen lives have been

lost. All the needless bloodshed is celebrated and praised as we make our way to the dining hall to feast in their honor.

The four victors are seated at the royal table, their injuries only barely treated as they scarf down their meal like it might be their last. And it very well could be. King Cepheus toasts the families that lost their children, reminding them of the honor in their sacrifices.

Across the room, I catch sight of Lady Palakiko.

Sadness radiates from her entire being. Her husband smiles, though it is strained. He raises his glass to the king, but she sits rigid in her chair. Something passes between them, and with trembling fingers, she finally raises her glass as well.

But, beneath the table, they are squeezing each other's hands so tightly their knuckles are white—grounding one another like anchors in a tumultuous sea. It could be grief, but it feels like something more fierce than that.

And why shouldn't they be angry? They are just as helpless when it comes to the whims of the king as the rest of us are. For the first time today, I wonder if the twelve men who died today actually volunteered, or if they were chosen.

He will not win. Not this time.

I cling to those words, tugging them to me and wrapping myself in them, allowing myself to take the meager comfort they offer.

For me, and for everyone hurt by the senseless games of tyrants.

CHAPTER THIRTY-EIGHT

MELODI

Gliding from one corner of my room to the other, I try to calm my raging thoughts. I try even harder not to look at the door that separates my room from Ari's.

The temptation to go to him tonight is greater than usual, like it's gnawing at my bones and setting my skin on fire, torturing me to suffer from his absence the way all those men today suffered for my presence.

It was just a little less unbearable when I thought they had a choice, but now...

In a desperate move to distract myself, I pull some seaweed from the side tray, hastily throwing together memorials. I'm so lost in the familiar actions of weaving the seaweed into intricate patterns that I miss the telltale thrumming in my veins, the instant relief that signifies Ari's arrival.

"They do not deserve your memorials, Kala, when they were fighting for the right to own you against your will."

He is closer to me than he usually stands, the heat from his chest emanating to my back.

His wording strikes me as interesting. Own me against my will, as opposed to owning me with my permission.

Isn't that what Ari does?

I spin around to face him, and for once, he doesn't move away. Has the day worn on him the same way it has me? The constant threat of me belonging to someone else when it feels so impossibly wrong to belong to anyone but Ari.

Just as he belongs to me.

I know this like I know my own soul, and he is getting worse at hiding the fact that he knows it, too.

I haven't bothered to shield my thoughts since he walked in. Some part of me recognizes that I'm trying to goad him into action, into speaking, acknowledgement, literally anything but this gut-wrenching, infuriating game we've been playing.

His hands clench at his sides, but I don't back down. My shields are stronger, now. He has no need to hide this anymore.

Slowly, I lean forward, pulled toward him as surely as a fish caught on a line.

"Kala." The word is a warning.

A demand.

A plea.

And I ignore it, all the same, crushing my mouth against his.

Whatever self-control he has been holding fast to dissolves the moment our lips meet. Lightning surges between us, a heat that burns deeply from his soul to mine. Instead of sating the part of me that all but begs for him, this kiss only illuminates the yawning void he hasn't yet filled.

This is right. I know it is.

We are supposed to be this way, his skin on mine, his mind melding against my own.

His hands snake around my back, fingertips digging into my skin as he tugs me even closer to deepen the kiss. His tongue presses against the seam of my lips, parting them so he can taste me.

I don't hesitate before opening them further, his tongue dancing against mine to a symphony only we can hear. Fireworks explode behind my eyes, reverberating through my body at each point of contact.

A dam has broken and all I know, all I can see and feel and taste is him. He glides me back against the wall, his mouth never breaking contact with mine—claiming me just as surely as I have wanted to claim him.

He shifts his attention to my neck, his lips and tongue leaving a trail of fire in their wake. I can hardly breathe.

"Tell me what this is," I say as my hands snake up his arms, latching around his neck and toying with the ends of his silken waves. "Please."

On that word, his walls come crashing down.

I see everything, then.

The moment I hit the water, when my thoughts came cascading into his. The surge of ownership, of protection, of pure, unadulterated longing that he was so unprepared for, even when he had long since figured out who I was to him.

The dance. The way he almost murdered the man who dared to approach me.

A song. *The* song. The same haunting melody that I heard for weeks, pulsing through him, leading him to the cliffs just outside my window. The moment that he saw my face in the tower. The recognition.

Each agonizing moment since we've been here, tinged with fear and panic and *want*. His sleepless nights. His unending frustration.

It's all open to me, a barrage of emotion and memories I seem to be pulling directly from his mind. I greedily sort through them, looking for the word. The definition. The confirmation.

And finally, there it is. A conversation with a woman I don't recognize, bits and phrases flitting from his mind.

What if we were in control of who she married?

I freeze.

You would force her?

No.

I won't have to.

A knife lances through me. By the time I find what I've been looking for, I have already pulled away. All this time, all this wondering for a word that feels so right and now, so stars-damned bittersweet.

He scrambles to put his shields in place, but it's too late. I tilt my head up just in time to see the guilt swimming in his eyes as the final part of the conversation clicks into place.

Soulmate.

CHAPTER THIRTY-NINE

MELODI

Soulmate.

I repeat the word in my head, once, then twice.

I can barely process the waves of emotion crashing over me. Elation and a feeling of rightness because I finally know with a certainty that he feels our bond as wholly as I do, that it isn't going anywhere.

But all of that relief is tempered by another stab of betrayal when I remember the conversation I witnessed— the conversation he accidentally let slip.

"Kala—"

"No." It's one word, but final.

I can't control the visceral way I am reacting to this any more than I can control anything else around Ari. This bond—this *soulmate* bond, seems to take my choices away as surely as the people around me do.

Ari winces, slamming his shields into place. I almost feel guilty before I remember that he jumped in the boat of everyone else in my life who was high-handedly deciding who I should marry.

Somehow, that hurts the most.

I bring my shields up, too, shutting him out like he has so often done to me and swimming farther away from him.

"It must have been convenient for you, when you realized who I was, tying up your rebellion in one neat little package." The words are coated with more sadness than ire.

The Mayiman people truly do need this rebellion. They need to be free of my savage grandfather. They need stability.

I am not so selfish that I don't see that.

"It wasn't convenient," Ari all but growls. "And that wasn't for the rebellion. It was for you."

He moves forward but I hold up a hand to stop him. "Another move to keep me safe without involving me."

"It was too dangerous."

That word ignites a fire in my veins. "This is my fight, too. Don't you think that I care about the people, too? That I feel some responsibility that it's my family, once again, making everyone around us suffer?"

His jaw clenches. "I know that, but—"

"Were you even going to ask me?" I cut him off, still trying to land on the part of this that hurts the most.

"Was I going to ask you if you wanted to be with me?" he asks, a note of incredulity to his tone—and something else. Something deeper.

I nod.

ELLE MADISON & ROBIN D MAHLE

"It didn't occur to me that I needed to." He has wiped every trace of emotion from both his face and his voice, not even allowing them to leak out through our bond. Our soulbond.

My teeth grind together. Obviously, it didn't occur to him that he needed to ask me, or even inform me. Doesn't he see that that's the problem?

Of course, I want to be with him, but I didn't even have all of the information to make a decision about the rest of our lives, didn't even know it was an option. All my life, I have been silenced, and my choices have been made for me.

Now, this.

It's not that I would have said no. I'm not even sure I *could* have said no. But to hear him so dismissively reference the rest of my life like it's a foregone conclusion he came to because he has had such unfettered access to my soul's obsession with his...

I need time to process it all without him overhearing each of my thoughts.

I force myself not to look at his perfect features or his swollen lips or the hair I just had my hands clenched in. Force myself not to think about the comfort I could find in his arms, or the warmth of his body on mine. Force myself not to cave.

"You should go back to your room now," I say evenly, though tears stab at the back of my eyes.

"Kala—" he starts to protest, but I cut him off.

"I need space, Ari. Can you just...give me that? Please?" My voice breaks on the echo of the word that started this all.

A muscle ticks in his strong jaw and his fists clench at his sides. Finally he dips his head in one, simple nod, before returning to his rooms.

CHAPTER FORTY

ARIIHAU

It's my most restless night since the day Kane first dragged her into the water. All night, I'm plagued with a mixture of hurt and remorse. It doesn't help that she's doing the one thing I've been begging her to do since we met—keeping her walls in place.

She's more determined than ever to lock me out, and I can't feel a single thought through the bond.

Does she honestly feel like the soulmate bond is a cage?

And seas, can I even blame her?

Time and time again, I have watched people suffer for their soulmate bonds. Growing up in the palace has given me an up close view I could have just as soon lived without.

Didn't it feel like a curse to me, at first, also? When all I had wanted was to eradicate this royal line, to free my people, only to discover that she was the one person I could never bring myself to hurt.

Even if all of Mayim paid the price.

Still, I have only ever seen one person deny the bond, and that was before it was sealed. It's unheard of for someone to walk away after. Though the king's children and nieces and nephews suffered unspeakable horrors for their bonds, especially those who were unfortunate enough to bond with someone outside the nobility, they still chose to suffer that fate rather than be separated from their mate.

I would never wish that for Kala, but when he was no longer around to torment us...

No.

It never occurred to me that she wouldn't want to be with me when we were able to, free of her grandfather's tyranny. But it's sure as seas occurring to me now, twisting my insides and eating me alive.

I swim laps around my room until dawn. Every other hour, Napo tried to drag me to bed, but I couldn't sit still enough to rest. He then took to lobbing tiny shells in my direction to try to make me stop.

That didn't work either.

By the time I answer Kane's knock at the door, I'm bleary-eyed and still in yesterday's armor. He raises an eyebrow at my state.

"I would ask if you were up all night having fun, but you look like a dead blobfish."

I glare at him, but it doesn't have the same effect it would on another Warrior. Kane only smirks back.

I throw up a rude gesture and he laughs, shutting the door behind him. A minute later, I find myself telling him the truth, just as I have since I was a child.

"If by fun, you mean hearing my own soulmate say she didn't want to be with me, then sure."

He gives me a disbelieving look. "Having heard Kala's many and varied lustful thoughts about you, I have a hard time seeing that. Did she say she didn't want to be with you?"

I think back to the specifics that I've been playing over again in my mind.

"She was angry that I told Lani we would be together...after, and she thought about how both the bond and I are controlling arseweeds."

He scoffs, knowing full well that isn't exactly what she said.

"Well, you are a controlling arseweed, but I happen to find it one of your more endearing qualities. And so does she—don't pretend you haven't heard her thoughts on the matter—though her sentiments lean in an entirely different direction than mine." He smirks again before continuing in a more serious tone. "But you have to remember that she isn't from here. She knows nothing about the bond. She has been given no choices, not before, and not now."

I look away. We've both heard her thoughts about her life before, locked away in silence and promised to a man she hates. Is that what this feels like for her?

"No," he says flatly. "And for seas' sake, get your thoughts under control before you get us all killed. If I'm going to die for the cause, I'd rather it not be for the tantrum you're throwing, at least."

Kala is watching the games closely.

Kala. I repeat the title again. What had started as a way to distance myself from her, a way to keep her at arm's length has now become an endearment.

Melodi. I test her name a little louder through our bond, trying to grab her attention.

It's stupid. Selfish. *Dangerous.*

But it doesn't matter since she's doing a rather admirable job at locking me out of her mind. I can't deny that it's impressive how quickly she has learned to protect her thoughts. I only wish she had learned earlier—before I grew used to her voice in my head. Before I became addicted to it. *Craved it.*

Kala'ni Danica gives me a warning look and I realize that even though my shields are where they should be, my eyes are not.

I haven't paid an ounce of attention to the battles. I couldn't say who has won or lost, or even list the names of the current contenders. But I know how many times Kala's fingers have twitched. How many times her long lashes have kissed her cheeks as she blinked.

The bond is angry and desperate, and it's making me careless.

I can't afford to take these risks now, not when we are so close to being free of Cepheus. Kane told me that Lani sent word that the rebels are to strike the day after tomorrow.

And I'll be ready when they do.

It's an effort to force my attention away from my soulmate and back on the arena, but I finally manage just in time for the next four contenders to be called.

Nino is one of them.

He glances up at Kala, and I have to remind myself that he is on our side, one of the many contingency plans we have in place in case the rebellion fails. My last line of defense to protect her from the others who would take her as their bride.

He would never force himself on her. She is safe from him, even if the bond tries to tell me otherwise.

It won't come to that, though. In two days' time, we will end this. The king's reign of terror will be over and Melodi will be free to choose whatever life she wants. Even if it doesn't include me.

And I will have to find a way to live with that.

CHAPTER FORTY-ONE

MELODI

a dozen more men are dead, and four winners are added to the ranks to fight another day.

I force myself to keep my shields in place all day, even though the pounding in my skull is beginning to make my eye twitch. As much as I hate that Ari was right to keep things from me, it takes everything I have to keep the king out of my mind, to keep *that word* from running through my head.

I would not have been capable, even a week ago. I am barely capable now.

The only relief comes when I let them down long enough to respond to simple questions, or to congratulate the victors at dinner.

Once again, the families of the dead are relegated to a table of honor, even though there is nothing honorable in making them hide their grief and feast and celebrate the people who murdered their children.

Danica invites me to join her in her rooms after

ELLE MADISON & ROBIN D MAHLE

dinner, though it feels less like an invitation and more like an order.

Which is just as well. I wouldn't have refused her. I'm not ready to be alone in my room on the other side of Ari. His presence as he escorts me to her chambers is overwhelming enough, though he doesn't so much as look at me.

When the door shuts behind us, Danica gestures toward the long sofa in her sitting room. I take a seat and watch her fill two goblets with dark purple jellies before she joins me.

She takes a drink, and I follow suit, relishing the small bursts of flavor. It reminds me of a rich, dry red wine, earthy and wooded, with notes of cocoa. It warms me from the inside out, the same way my favorite vintage did at the chateau.

"You don't have to choose him," she says, abruptly breaking the silence in my mind.

I freeze, my gaze meeting hers. Does she mean whoever wins these games? Or does she know somehow what transpired between me and Ari? She subtly glances toward the hallway where Ari stands guard on the other side of the door, and my insides twist.

There is no point in denying it now. All I can do is hope she will keep my secrets, as she has.

"That's not how I understood it," I say.

Her mouth flattens into a terse line, reminding me more of my mother than she ever has before.

"The soulmates were thought to be a gift from the dragons, providing the royal line with the means to find their perfect match," she explains, leaving me to fill in the obvious conclusion.

That it doesn't always feel that way.

"Everyone in the royal line?" I ask.

She raises an eyebrow. "Yes, my father has a soulmate."

I don't miss her use of the present tense, but it's a baffling thought.

"We did not know it was possible to reject the soulmate bond, but when my father killed Natia's husband and their daughter to rid her of any *complications*, she vowed never to forgive him. She said she would rather die than be bound to a monster."

Natia.

The woman from the cage. The one whose hand he took. I think back to him grabbing at his limb like there was a phantom pain. The venom with which she looked at him. The lack of fear.

"Is she your mother?" I ask, trying and failing to keep the horror from my tone.

"No. Cepheus took only concubines to bear his children when he could not have Natia. He killed them after, so we would not get too attached."

"Did it drive him insane? Being separated from his soulmate?" The thought is barely a whisper.

Would she be to blame if it were? The kingdom would have paid the price, but was it her responsibility to give her life to a man like him?

"Weren't you listening, child?" Danica cuts my stream of thought off. "I said you do not have to choose him. It is possible to be separate from your soulmate. The emptiness will still be there, but the urgency will fade, with great distance."

I don't ask her how she knows it's possible. She said all of the royal line had soulmates, yet I have never seen a trace of hers.

"I did what I had to in order to keep him safe," she confirms. "So as I said. This is not a choice you need to make. You can go back on land."

I consider her words. I don't have to choose Ari.

Only when those words sink in do I realize how badly I *want* to choose him. It isn't just the bond that draws me to him. It's his subtle sense of humor, the warmth he hides underneath his gruff exterior. It's the way he is willing to work against a man no one has ever beaten, a man who is backed by the might of a dragon itself, just to give his fellow people a better life.

No. I don't *have* to choose Ari. But given the option, I would, every time.

Danica looks inexplicably sad, shaking her head subtly. Then she says something to me that no one ever has before.

"You truly are your mother's daughter."

CHAPTER FORTY-TWO

MELODI

*A*ny doubt I have about what happened to my father is gone, evaporated in the wake of my aunt's proclamation.

She stares at me for so long with so much sorrow that I wonder if she will say anything else at all, or if she too is lost to her memories and whatever fragile sanity my family possesses.

"Father always knew," she says suddenly. "When the others sealed their bond."

I get just enough from her to know what that sealing entails, enough to tell me why Ari has been so careful about keeping his distance even when want overtakes us both.

"But Ursula was careful," my aunt goes on. "And so, so brilliant."

It's jarring to hear anyone speak of my mother with genuine affection in their tone.

"Then how did he find out?" I ask gently.

"She trusted the wrong person." Danica's face pinches with far more than simple grief.

It's guilt, thick, and potent, clouding the water around us like the crimson sea of blood from the day the rebels attacked.

She sighs and closes her eyes, then images appear in my mind. Memories.

Cepheus corners her, his lips pulled back in a snarl. Fear that radiates off of her and only fuels him more.

"Tell me the truth, and I will spare her."

She has watched so many of her other siblings die. She can't lose Ursula, too.

Finally, a shaky confession. Then Mother's shattered, ruined expression, like all the joy and hope and happiness has left her. Like she has been engulfed by flames that will never burn out and never have the mercy to end her.

"He tortured her?" I ask.

"He tortured Makani. For weeks. And she refused to shield herself from that pain out of penance. Whatever we shared in the womb, she always seemed to have taken more than her share of our bravery."

Again, there's a wistful, fond note to her voice, but it's gone as quickly as it came.

"Then my father finally killed Makani, and it broke what was left of Ursula. She left the next day. I never understood why she didn't take her own life as so many in her place did."

My aunt looks at me.

"And now I know why. She left to protect you."

The thought rings truer than I expect it to. She is a

strange balance of cruel and protective. She always has been. Memories assault me, whipping around my head with the force of hurricane winds.

Mother, her hands on my face, her features almost gentle.

This is for the best, she had said about Damian.

Of course, it would feel that way to her. She must have known I would have a soulmate. She would have seen that as a curse, something to protect me from, especially when her father was still the king.

I think of the moments of pride she had with my sisters, her insistence on being called Mother. Some part of her wanting, needing the family that she never got to have.

Then I remember the other side of her.

The side that sent a woman and her child into the shark infested water for a single perceived slight. The drain in the floor of her dungeons to capture the blood of her victims. Her children. Death after gruesome death at her feet. Rose's body, her face swollen and purple. Zaina's empty eyes. Aika's deadly hands. Damian's sadistic smirk.

And through it all, the endless rage and pain and grief that shines through everything my mother does.

How will she punish them now, if they fail? Will I lose all of my siblings as my aunt has lost hers?

"Oh, Ulla." Danica brings her hand to her mouth, horror widening her eyes. "What have you become?"

I meet her eyes in our moment of shared grief, perhaps the only two people in the world who still hold something other than disdain for the woman who gave me life.

I understand her, in a convoluted way I almost wish I didn't. Driven mad by the death of her soulmate. Clutching at power to protect the people she loves and punish the people she deems deserving.

I can't hate her, not anymore. But neither can I forgive her for the things she's done. The things she will still do. All while I sit here, powerless to stop her.

"You may be powerless, but I am not." My aunt's words are filled with a quiet steel I have never heard from her before.

For a rare change, her shields are down, and I feel all the pieces clicking together. A decision washes over her, settling into the marrow of her bones.

She has seen what her father became. For too many years, she has watched every member of her family succumb to violence and brutality, in one form or another. She has watched them tear each other and themselves apart, drowning in the destruction she felt like she was too weak to stop.

Danica can't reach Mother, not physically, but not mentally either. Not now. There is only one thing she can realistically contribute to.

"I would never ask you to do this," I say.

She nods solemnly. "The sister I knew was brilliant and calculating, but she would have died before hurting the people she loved. She would not have wanted to become this. And I have failed her once already."

I think about my own sisters, the way I have come so close to losing them both to the darkness inside of them. Could I have made the choice to end one of their lives, to save them from destroying themselves and the people around them?

I love them enough to know the answer, even if it would decimate pieces of myself to see it through.

So I don't argue with Danica again. Instead, I ask a more practical question.

"What about your father?"

She levels a look at me, more reminiscent of her usual self. "I am not blind, child, and neither are you. I think we both know he won't be long for this throne, or this world."

I raise my eyebrows. "Then why did you tell me I could leave Ari?"

She gives the closest thing to a shrug I have seen from her. "Because it was still your choice. Then and now."

I feel a surge of affection for this woman who has protected me and helped me since I arrived, at constant risk to herself. She is by no means immune to the king's wrath, but she took this on herself.

My mother didn't take her sister's share of the bravery. Not by half.

A small, sad smile graces Danica's lips. "I will leave tonight, and have my maid make excuses for me in the morning."

"Thank you," I tell her, hoping she understands the way I mean it to apply not just to this moment, or to her help with my sisters, but to everything she has done for me.

Somehow, I suspect this will be the last chance I have to tell her. I think when Danica leaves this palace, she might never look back. She doesn't argue with my last thought, though I know she hears it.

She only reaches out a hand to my shoulder in a display of affection.

"Goodbye, Melodi."

CHAPTER FORTY-THREE

MELODI

The next day is an echo of the ones before. More death. More bloodshed. More celebrations. I didn't talk to Ari last night. Or rather, he didn't talk to me. He's giving me the space I asked for. It's just as well. I needed last night to think, to process without anyone else sharing in my thoughts.

It's true that I would have chosen Ari, had he asked me. But he didn't ask me. It still bothers me that he doesn't see why that's a problem, but I finally feel like I'm in a place to explain it to him.

And I need to. I need him, us, to be solid, when everything else is spinning out of control.

I feel like I'm on a precipice, balancing on the edge of the world with only tragedy and grief to catch me when I fall. I don't know if my aunt will be able to help my sisters. I don't know if I'll ever see them again. If anyone will even get word to me if something happens to them.

I don't know if Mother will die, and if any part of me will mourn her loss when she does. But I do know that whatever this life brings me, I will find a way to spend it with Ari.

Or die at his side.

I push open the door between our rooms, quietly closing it behind me and leaning against the sandstone panes.

Ari looks up expectantly from where he is stretching in a warrior's pose, his tattoos writhing on his rippling muscles. Napo ceases his stretching as well, darting a knowing glance back and forth between us before quickly swimming out the window.

Ari ignores him entirely, his turquoise eyes transfixed on me.

"Kala?" he says my title like a question.

"Ariihau," I answer.

For all that I have thought about him, I don't know that I've ever said his name to him. His eyes widen, but his mind is still closed.

He solves that problem for me, though. In one fluid motion, he's upright, closing some of that distance between us. Even from a meter away, I can feel the heat of his body radiating to mine.

"I cannot live a life where I am silenced and kept in the dark," I tell him earnestly. "Not again."

He shakes his head, real pain in his features. "I would never do that to you."

"Maybe not intentionally," I allow. "But there I was, without the knowledge to make any kind of informed choices. Without the ability to voice an opinion. Just because you are in my head does not mean you can decide for yourself when I don't need a say."

I wait until I feel him accepting my words before I go on.

"I need to know that it won't happen again. No more secrets or half-truths or decisions for my own good."

He visibly wars with himself. "The things the king is capable of—"

"I know," I cut him off. "You know that I know."

His muscles go tight as he clenches his fists. "I couldn't bear it if something were to happen to you."

"Nor I you," I say pointedly. "I know that you want to protect me."

More than that, I know that he needs to protect me. That rejecting his protection would be rejecting him. I can sense it, now that I understand more of how the bond works.

"And I will always accept your protection," I go on. "But I am not a child, Ari, and I require your respect as well."

He looks up in shock. "Of course, I respect you."

I don't break his gaze, willing him to see the connection as I see it. Minutes pass in silence, but it doesn't bother me. It's not an empty, broken, yawning void like the silence of my childhood.

It's draped against the backdrop of Ari's constantly working mind, all the pieces of our story he is rearranging and putting together in light of the things I have finally been able to bring myself to say.

"All right, Kala. No more secrets," he says, entwining our fingers together.

"Even if you feel it's dangerous," I press.

A wave of grief passes over his features, like he has

seen my death already, and I am asking him to let it stand. But he gives me a sharp nod, letting his walls crash down around us.

I feel his pain and his acceptance and his honesty, the way he would stop at nothing for me, even this. Even though it's killing him.

"On my honor," he says at last, pulling our linked fingers against his lips in a gesture that is both proprietary and unexpectedly sweet, like he needs to touch me.

Like he savors it.

Relief weakens my knees, tears stabbing at the back of my eyes.

"Then tell me everything," I say.

So he does.

CHAPTER FORTY-FOUR

MELODI

By the time I am finished sorting through the torrent of memories and emotions and plans that Ari has revealed to me, there's one thought running endlessly through my head.

It's not enough time.

I sink down onto his bed, my mind reeling.

Tomorrow, the rebels will attack, and Ari will lead them.

I want to have faith in him. I *do* have faith in him. The fates have been cruel already, though, and all I can see is my sisters and my soulmate and even my aunt, all running to their deaths while I stand by and slowly go insane from the grief of it all.

I can't change that.

I can't ask him not to do this when so many lives are at stake, his own included. We won't be able to hide this bond forever, and there's nowhere we can escape that Cepheus can't find us. We need this rebellion. The people need it. Danica needs it.

All of that is beyond my control, but there is one thing that isn't.

I can make sure Ari understands how I feel. That he is bolstered by whatever protection and love and peace a fully sealed bond will give him.

"Ask me now," I say softly, intruding upon his similarly racing thoughts.

He looks down at me, hope and relief warring for dominance in his fathomless sea-green eyes.

He stands in front of me, cupping my face in his massive hand. His thumb gently trails from my forehead to my chin, his fingers threading through my hair.

"Melodi." His voice reverberates in the deepest part of my mind, the private place that is reserved for him alone.

It's just my name, but already, tears burn my eyes.

"Will you consent to share your life and your body and your mind with me? Will you belong to me as wholly as I belong to you now?"

My entire being reacts to his words. Shivers race along my skin, anticipation thrumming between us until it becomes something almost painful, this encompassing need to say yes. It doesn't feel like I'm being coerced by the bond, though, or like I'm out of control.

It just feels like the part of me that knows in my soul that Ari is my perfect match, begging me to let us both feel whole.

"Yes," I say, letting him feel the certainty in my response.

It's a risk, knowing Cepheus—and everyone else—will be able to sense it if we seal the bond. But one way or another, things will be over tomorrow, and I will not let them end with us apart.

Ari's thoughts mirror mine, his desire mingling along with my own as his hand trails down my arm, lighting my skin on fire everywhere he touches. There is a question in his thoughts, a request for permission.

"Yes," I say again.

Our first kiss was rushed, frenzied, almost defiant.

This one is agonizingly slow. Ari starts with his lips at my forehead, then he traces a gentle arc down to my lips. Warmth spreads down to my toes, awareness coursing through my body as I arch into him.

He moves further against me, one muscled arm bracing himself on either side of mine as he guides me down onto the bed. Then his lips are on my jaw, my neck, my collarbone, and I am lost to a tumultuous sea of want and need and a rightness that aches down into my core.

But Ari is there with me, anchoring me even as his thoughts are an endless, intoxicating mirror of my own desire.

His hands are sure and steady, igniting me even as they cradle me with more gentleness than I would have thought the massive warrior was capable of.

If I expected to feel fear or hesitation, there is neither when he slides my dress over my head, exploring every inch of skin he reveals. He takes his time, giving me space to run my fingers and my lips along the ridges and tattoos and scars that adorn his perfect body.

We spend the night bolstering ourselves and each other, losing ourselves in the endless rightness of the bond and trying to steel ourselves against everything to come.

But when morning arrives, I am still not prepared.

CHAPTER FORTY-FIVE

ARIIHAU

I know something is wrong when Moli doesn't come to dress Kala in the morning.

Kala returned to her room in the early hours of the morning, though it killed me to be separated from her—not physically, now that the bond is sealed, but because she belongs at my side. I didn't sleep after she left. Instead, I spent the time preparing, donning my armor, sharpening the blades of my trident.

But the rebels aren't due to attack until breakfast. And Kane should be here to relieve Noa. It's part of our plan.

Not wanting to alarm my soulmate unnecessarily, I slip into the hallway with Napo at my side. The feeling of wrongness is more pervasive here, raising the hairs along the back of my neck.

It's silent, and the water is far too still.

Napo clings to my leg as if he can sense it too, his round eyes flitting back and forth between Noa and Kala's door behind her. The lieutenant looks on edge, too, standing more rigidly than normal.

"Commander," she says more tentatively than usual, standing at attention.

From a rare, brief glimpse at her thoughts, I discern that her hesitation is equal parts concern for an unusual situation and an odd combination of emotions regarding the things she apparently overheard last night.

We have no time to deal with that now, though. Before I can so much as return Noa's greeting, Melodi appears in the doorway.

The rosy hue is gone from her cheeks, last night's desire replaced with the same apprehension that's overtaken me.

What is it? she asks through the bond.

I don't know yet.

"Lieutenant Noa, have you heard from Kane this morning?" I ask her.

He was supposed to protect Melodi while I met up with Lani and the others before the attack. It would have kept the king from noticing our bond preemptively, but now... I can't very well send her with only the young warrior. It would be more suspicious, not to mention dangerous for everyone.

Noa's voice pulls me back to the present, confusion and trepidation mingling in her tone when she speaks.

"I have not, Commander," she trails off for a moment. "Actually, I have not yet heard from anyone today."

Anyone?

Every fiber of my being is on alert as I glide to the rooms across the hall, not even bothering to knock before throwing the doors open. All of them are empty.

There are no servants darting around. No warriors

standing guard. No voices. No slipstreams, or rippling of the water. *Nothing.* A wave of panic swells inside of me.

Where the hell is Kane?

I war with myself for a moment, deciding what the next steps should be.

A very primal part of me wants to lock Kala in her room. To arm her with my trident and tell her to hide until I can find him, until we can escape to the rebel colony. If everything has gone to hell, though, it will take longer to come back to her. Seas only know what her grandfather might have planned.

One look in her amethyst gaze tells me she wouldn't agree to that anyway. And after everything, all she wants is a say. She deserves that much.

She nods once, and I realize she has heard each of my thoughts through our bond.

Without waiting another second, I grab her hand, ordering Noa to follow us as we wind our way down one hall after another. Napo moves from my leg to wrap himself around Melodi, his tentacles enveloping her torso protectively as his inky eyes scan for danger.

Each hall we pass is as empty as the first. We don't swim past a single Mayima.

I run through a list of possibilities in my mind to account for the absence of literally everyone in the palace. Did the games begin earlier today? That wouldn't account for the servants missing as well.

Did the king call for a meeting and we weren't invited? Is he planning something more than just marrying Melodi off to the survivor of the games?

Does he know?

239

That last question ricochets through me, making my blood run cold. Dread pools in my chest, and I tug her closer to me.

No one should have been able to sense the bond until last night, but don't I know better than anyone that the king always knows more than he lets on? It was always unusual that he assigned me to be her guard when I normally lead patrols outside of the palace.

Unusual that although Melodi let her thoughts slip more often than not, he never once commented on it.

Seas damned hell.

The king's low laugh echoes through my mind, stopping me in my tracks. Kala hears it too, her hand trembling in mine.

Noa brings her bronze trident up higher, scanning the space around us.

"It could be a trap," Noa whispers, and I nod.

It most certainly is. I can already smell the blood—metallic like the hull of a thousand rusted ships. Like lost chests full of coins, slowly corroding in the briny sea.

How much has been spilled for the smell to be that strong?

"Come now, don't keep us waiting," Cepheus says, and I wince.

It's Melodi who makes the next move, gliding forward and pulling me along behind her.

I glance from her to the passageway leading to the front doors. There are no warriors guarding them. We could escape now, get as far from here as possible. But then I think of my cousin. I think of the bloodstained water calling to us and wonder if some of it belongs to him.

If he's still alive, can I just leave him here without trying to get him out? Melodi squeezes my hand in answer.

Damn everything.

I swim forward, keeping her tucked carefully between myself and Noa. We round the corner, pushing open the massive doors to the dining hall. Red water washes over us—so thick that it's almost impossible to see through. A fog that only barely conceals the corpses lining the room.

Melodi gasps, and I pull her closer.

There are well over one hundred people here, nearly every member of the rebellion.

And all of them are dead.

CHAPTER FORTY-SIX

ARIIHAU

The bodies are anchored to the floor by chains. Their hands are bound together at their backs, so their lifeless eyes stare up at the ceiling, their mouths twisted in horror.

They did not die well. They did not die as warriors. They weren't even given the dubious courtesy of an honorable death. Swallowing back the bile rising in my throat, I scan the room for signs of life.

Panic grips me, and I study each of the faces again, making sure my cousin isn't among them.

"My king," I say as evenly as possible, trying to buy us some time. "What has happened?"

Another dark chuckle echoes from the shadows, along with the sound of a chain scraping lightly against the floors.

I can sense the king, his looming presence lurking closer by the second, but I can't see him yet. Straining my senses, I feel two others, as well, the faint whisper of consciousness. The crimson water is hiding them well.

There's a rippling in the water. Cepheus glides forward like a shadow, an omen of death. His expression is entirely too satisfied.

And in his hand is a chain.

A small anchor is attached to the bottom, keeping whatever is attached to it from floating away. My fist tightens around my trident, but I don't dare make a move —not when I don't know what he's playing at, or how I'm going to get Melodi to safety.

"Apparently," Cepheus finally answers, casting a disdainful glance at Lani's corpse. "There was a coup planned for later this very day."

Melodi stiffens beside me, but her shields are firmly in place as he continues.

"You'll be relieved to know my men found the traitors before any damage could be done." His deep purple eyes finally lock onto mine. "They took care of it while you were busy...*protecting* my granddaughter."

My pulse drums a furious beat in my temples. He knows. We knew he would sense the bond, but it's more than that. He isn't surprised.

More than that, he knows I was involved with the rebels. He knows, and he's playing a game.

"The honor was mine," I reply carefully.

I need to get us out of here, but I need to find Kane first and that means stalling for time. "I know who she is to you—what she means to the people. I will do everything I can to keep her alive and safe."

A long pause weighs down the room. Cepheus' eyes narrow, his grin going feral.

"Good," he says. "You can imagine my surprise when

my top commander hadn't heard a single word about this rebellion. But I suppose that can be forgiven, considering your recent change in position."

He glides forward another step, the chain scraping against the floor behind him. I still can't see what he's dragging, and I'm not sure I want to.

My eyes drift instead to Lani's corpse.

Her body is easily the most damaged. Her limbs are shattered in multiple places, her jaw broken, her clothes ripped. The king stares at her with something like a sick, twisted satisfaction. I have no doubt he did this to her, himself. That he enjoyed it.

By the looks of it, she's been dead for hours. They all have. Hours...while I was distracted.

Kala squeezes my hand and I feel the reassurance through our bond.

Not your fault.

Isn't it though?

She squeezes my hand again, but this time, it's a spike of panic through the bond.

Kane, she whispers his name, her eyes fixed on the king, or rather, on the place just behind him. He is finally close enough that we can see what it is he's been dragging.

Another body, attached to another chain floating in the water just behind him.

My cousin.

Rage and panic swim through my veins, choking out all rational thought.

I need to know if he's still alive. His skin is pale, and his nose is broken, bruises already forming under his eyes.

His arms are bound and twisted in a way that tells me they are surely broken as well.

Yet, if I listen carefully, I can hear the faint sound of a ragged heartbeat. The king looks up at Kane, then back at me, his grin stretching even wider.

"This one assures me you had nothing to do with it, but I know how people lie to protect the ones they love."

He is ostensibly talking about my cousin, but his icy stare goes from me to Melodi. I freeze.

Warriors train from infancy, not just to fight, but to regulate our emotions. So though I have faced death more times than I can count, though I have seen battles and bloodshed enough for several lifetimes, I have never before known terror as I know it in this moment.

We played this all wrong.

Now, Melodi will pay the price.

CHAPTER FORTY-SEVEN

REMY

From the moment my brother died, it's felt as though I was living my life in a series of stolen moments scattered like stars amongst the stark backdrop of my own mortality.

But I've never felt that as keenly as I do now, watching my wife and her monkey, the strange pieces of this life we've started to build.

Aika plays with one of her throwing stars, idly flipping it in the air and catching it, while Pumpkin sleeps on her shoulder, buried underneath the silken waterfall of her onyx hair.

For all that I have thought I wanted revenge, looking at her now makes me realize it's so much more than that.

If I believed we would be safe from Madame, I would walk away now and take Aika with me and never look back. We could live out our lives, protecting our people and adopting some of the orphans away from all of this, even if it meant the person who hurt my family would walk free.

But Madame will never let that happen.

So I study the map and the three other people seated at the table, listening as Zaina explains that we might be able to fashion some sort of weapon since Madame bested Khijhana relatively easily before.

And that was when we had the element of surprise, which we will be lacking in if Khijhana accompanies us to shore. The enormous cat is a lot of things, but stealthy is not one of them.

"We still need to take out Damian first," Aika says, catching her star and sheathing it in one swift movement.

My fists clench at the name of the man who killed my father. Who kidnapped my wife, and wants to do far worse to her.

"Unless he's also part Mayima, that shouldn't be a problem," Einar says, his voice nearly as furious as I feel.

Aika and her sister exchange a look, the latter subtly shaking her head.

"As much as it pains me to admit this," Zaina says. "It would be a mistake to underestimate him. He's ruthless and brilliant and unhinged in his devotion to Madame."

My wife nods her agreement. Which is noteworthy in and of itself, since she and Zaina agree approximately once every six to seven weeks.

"He doesn't set the limits for himself that most people do," Aika adds. "And he fights even dirtier than I do."

"Yes, he plays mind games," Zaina picks back up, taking a sip from Einar's whiskey glass. "He's a master at distracting people while he attacks."

"Is that how he bested you before?" Einar is a braver

man than I am for asking that of his temperamental wife, but she doesn't look offended.

"No," she says evenly. "He's just a better fighter than I am, and twice my size. Even Aika can't beat him every time."

Aika looks irritated, but reluctantly contributes her own experience. "He *did* play mind games in my case. But Zaina isn't wrong. In an even spar, I would only beat him half the time. We will need to plan on two of us to take him down."

My brows furrow and I pour myself another glass of whiskey. "If he's so skilled, why were you chosen to be the Flame?"

The room goes still and Aika inspects my features warily.

"Don't ask questions you don't want the answer to," she cautions.

I understand her hesitation. The Flame was Madame's enforcer, known for a staggeringly high body count and the general terror they instilled in the underbelly of Bondé.

But I meant what I said all those weeks ago in our rooms.

"I love all of you, remember?" I remind her. "No matter what."

She relaxes incrementally.

"Well, there's the obvious." She gestures to herself. "The intimidation factor, the surprise of me being this tiny, unexpectedly terrifying thing for them. But besides that, I was ruthless in a different way than Damian is. He gets distracted by his baser instincts, whereas I was just her obedient soldier."

She looks sideways at Zaina, and something starts turning in the back of my mind.

"I think it's more than that," I say quietly and three sets of eyes fix on me. "She might have a weakness for her children, but she plays favorites. That's why it was so easy for you to blame Damian for as long as you did. We can find a way to use that."

Einar's fist clenches around his glass, and I know he's already seeing the possibilities.

Seeing the possibilities, and hating them.

Still, a plan forms behind his eyes. I don't get a chance to push him on what it is before the alarm bells ring out for the second time in as many weeks.

Before any of us can react or even get up from our chairs, the door slides open and a tall, slim, horrifyingly familiar figure fills up the entire doorway.

Madame has found us.

CHAPTER FORTY-EIGHT

MELODI

A lifetime of Mother's horrors has been eclipsed by a single, bloodstained room.

Dead and broken bodies float in front of us, arranged throughout the room like some kind of macabre garden. Like trophies.

Did it take him hours? Did he do this alone to ensure that the visual he presented was just so? Just the right amount of shock and horror displayed so that it would have the ultimate effect when we entered the room?

Did he choose where to position each body? Who to display first?

Knowing what I do of the woman who raised me, I have to imagine he did. Much like my mother, everything the king does is intentional. And everything he says.

I know how people lie to protect those they love.

My heartbeat thunders in my ears, but it's not loud enough to drown out the echo of his words. Something in his tone tells me he has known all along who Ari and I were to each other. He has merely played a game, just as he did with Kane.

Kane.

Though he looks just as lifeless as the rest of the corpses around us, I know in my soul that he isn't dead. Cepheus could have killed him too, but right now, Kane is more useful to him alive—as leverage over Ari—than he would be dead. My grandfather will ensure whatever he has planned succeeds with the most damage possible.

Another skill he taught his daughter.

A tentacle wraps around my leg, and Napo buries his face in my hip while Ari's hand clutches mine even tighter.

The king's eyes flit back and forth between us and I am suddenly aware of each part of my skin that touches Ari's. The way I'm clinging to his arm. The protective stance he's taken.

"In light of this revelation," Cepheus over-emphasizes the word. "There will be a change to the games today. An addition to the contenders competing for your hand."

"I thought Warriors weren't allowed to compete," I say tentatively, and Cepheus tsks in response.

"Come now, Granddaughter, surely you have learned enough through your *studies* to know that doesn't matter when it comes to the mating bond. The bond chooses for us, regardless of station." There is an edge to his words, his hatred for the bond coming through with each syllable. "And I cannot imagine that our Commander here would object."

It's a challenge, and Ari doesn't hesitate, not even for a moment, before responding. "Of course not, my king."

Pride and fear run in equally vicious currents through my veins. Ari's shields are fully in place and his expression is neutral, but I can feel the rage coursing through him.

"Very well," Cepheus says, paying no mind to the victim behind him. "Then let us begin."

THE ARENA IS FILLED to the brim.

Nobles, warriors, and servants alike are seated in the stadium chairs, silent as the grave when we enter.

How long have they been waiting? Were they forced to move through the dining hall before they came here? Did they see all the death, and do they still have some of the blood lingering on their skin?

It would explain the silence. I wonder if any of them were part of the rebellion, if they wanted it to succeed. If Moli is among their number or if she was killed just for existing, like so many others in the king's orbit.

Killed because he suspected her of the smallest shred of kindness.

The atmosphere is charged, like it's primed and ready for a storm—waiting for that first bolt of lightning to strike. I just don't know yet where it will land. I feel the weight of the people's stares as we make our way to the royal box, the tension coursing through them as they bow their heads in greeting for their king. For me.

My throat burns, and a thousand spiders dance along my skin at their obeisance. I don't want to be linked to this monster in any way.

They sit stoically as the king announces the change of

plans, all the while displaying the broken body of one of his top warriors like a demented keepsake. Kane floats just above us, close enough that I can sense his feeble heartbeat, but far enough away that the sharks have already begun to circle. They're waiting for permission from the king to take his body as their next meal.

I want to be sick.

The only consolation I have is that Cepheus dismissed Noa to the stands. He has allowed her to live.

"We are going to do things differently today," the king begins, his voice grating on my mind like nails on a chalkboard. "I have decided to allow one final contender to enter the competition."

The crowd stirs. They shift in their seats uncomfortably, scanning the nobles being led into the arena. Ari is the last to enter and a collective gasp rings out.

"This will be the final battle," Cepheus continues, his grin widening. "May the best Mayima reign victorious."

Chills creep down my spine, covering my skin in goosebumps and hollowing me from the inside out.

Peace, Kala. Ari's voice wraps around me, and tears prick at my eyes. For the first time, the words fail to comfort me, but I try to find strength in them anyway.

There is nothing we can do but play along now. Even if it kills me to watch as every single competitor sets their sights on Ari, their first target already chosen.

The gong rings out.

The bloodshed begins anew.

CHAPTER FORTY-NINE

MELODI

*P*ain ricochets through my body, perfectly in sync with each blow Ari takes.

A spear slams longways against his back, and the pang explodes along my spine. Another stab of pain in my shoulder nearly sends me sailing from my seat. Silent tears stream out from my eyes into the open water.

Not for the pain itself, but because I know he is bearing it too, even more intensely.

I lock down my walls as much as I can, trying to keep this endless loop of agony from bouncing back to him. All I want to do is swim down to the arena and stop him from taking one more hit. To end this useless battle before another life is lost.

But I will not stew in my own feelings of uselessness when Ari fights on, so I resolve to find a way to be useful. I have a vantage point he doesn't, and a way to communicate with him that no one else can hear.

I watch the fight more closely, trying to pick up on things I normally wouldn't.

Ari moves through the pain as if he doesn't feel it at all. He attacks with a strength I have never seen before, taking down Mayima after Mayima, even when they circle like sharks who are desperate to devour him. All except for the silver-haired man who had looked at me before—Nino, Ari had told me. He hangs back a bit, taking the others out instead of Ari.

Which makes sense because he is on our side. Or he was. Now, there can only be one survivor. He can't be on Ari's side and his own, and I don't know which way he will land if it comes down to just them.

Napo clings to my leg, burying his face in my calf. His entire body is trembling in fear. I place a hand on his head, offering him what little comfort I can while sending Ari a few timely warnings through our bond. I try to be his eyes when he can't track them all at once.

Beneath you, I warn him of the two nobles trying to sneak up from the trench. He dodges out of the way just in time.

On your left.

Three more waiting near the reef.

King Cepheus turns his glare on me, studying my expression, the way I'm holding my ribcage after Ari takes another blow.

"I know what you're doing," he says, but I don't falter.

It hardly matters now. Noa shifts at my side, her fingers flexing around the staff of her trident. The move itself is innocuous enough, but I know what she's doing, what she's preparing for. And I know she will lose if she tries.

"Don't worry," Cepheus says. "Danica will get her

punishment as well, as soon as we have taken care of yours."

He's trying to distract me, and it almost works. But Danica isn't coming back. She's safer than we are right now.

I throw a private warning out to Ari. Another beat of silence passes before the king tries his tactics again.

"Will you cry the way she did?" This question finally breaks my concentration, if only for the random nature of it. "It was pathetic, really."

The way who did?

Disgust coats his expression. His violet eyes go distant as if in memory, and I belatedly realize he's referring to my mother, not Danica.

"Why?" I force the question out through my mental shields. "She was your child—"

"She was weak."

It's baffling that anyone would use that word to describe Mother. Madame. The terror of Corentin, the waking nightmare that haunts Delphine. Yet she is nothing more than a shadow of his cruelty.

Screwing my eyes shut, I try to think of some appropriate response, something that might stir any dormant residual benevolence he has left.

Or perhaps I just want to hurt him half as much as he has hurt everyone.

"Did you show weakness when you hurt your mate?" I force the image of Natia in the cage toward him. I focus on her missing hand, the bruises and the cold, lifeless stare of her eyes. Didn't he feel her pain? Can he still? "How could you bear—"

My question is cut off by a growl rippling through my mind.

Cepheus stands, stretching to his full height, and I can't help but scramble from my chair in panic. Napo releases my leg, alarm stretching his inky eyes into saucers as the king glides toward me in a lightning fast move.

My grandfather's grin stretches wide, and I know he's heard my thoughts. Then, his hand is around my neck as he slowly pushes me against the wall.

It's a power move I have seen Mother make too many times. And I have seen what follows as well. Watched as her grip tightens, as faces turn blue from the lack of oxygen. Watched her slowly bring them to the brink of death, before snapping their necks entirely.

Then a tentacle wraps around his face, followed by another and another. Napo is trying to wrench the king away from me, using half of his tentacles to blind him or tug at him, and the other half crash against Cepheus' face and shoulders and chest.

My vision begins to swim, tears stinging my eyes.

"Napo," I force the panicked word out through my shields. "Stop."

The octopus won't listen though and keeps hitting and biting my grandfather—who looks more annoyed than anything else. Without letting go of my neck, he reaches behind him and crushes Napo's body in a punishing grip. Napo's tentacles slacken and slide off of the king, who tosses him to the side like garbage.

"You will learn, child," he says, interrupting my raging thoughts. "That I will go to great lengths to get what I want. And right now, what I want are two things. Your silence. And your obedience. Am I understood?"

I test the walls of my mind, making sure that they are even more secure than before and dip my head into a slow nod. I don't let him hear the next thought, the one that echoes through me like a promise.

I hate you. I hate you. And I will find a way to end you.

He glides backward, the water rippling around him as a satisfied expression settles over his mouth. As soon as I can move, I'm at Napo's side, pulling his limp body into my arms. The skin around his eyes expand and contract for a moment, before they're wide open again.

He's alive.

"You are as weak as the rest of them." My grandfather practically spits out the words.

Something pulls his attention back down to the arena. He rushes to the window, the smile dying from his face. His eyes widen and scan whatever is happening below before a loud, booming laugh fills my head.

Panic runs claws over my skin, and I check the bond for Ari.

I can no longer feel his pain. I can't hear his thoughts.

Swallowing hard, I cautiously swim toward the open window, my gaze landing on the rippling muscles in his back as he raises his trident one final time. I want to feel relieved that he's still alive. Still fighting. But something else settles into my gut as I watch him hesitate.

There is only one fighter left.

The silver-haired Nino.

He's not fighting back. Instead, he presses his fist against his chest, an earnest expression in his pale gaze as he drops his sword and his trident. They slowly sink to the ground with a quiet, resounding thunk.

Defeat settles into Ari's shoulders, but he allows no more than the barest hesitation before running Nino through. Something inside of me breaks as I watch Ari slowly push Nino off of the trident and guide his body up to the waiting sharks.

Cepheus' laughter continues, and I wonder if something in his mind has completely snapped. It is the only sound in the arena, the only voice that dares to break the silence of those mourning their children. Of the victims that have been forced to watch the slaughter of the heirs to the noble houses.

I don't know what he has planned, but I am certain it has nothing to do with announcing Ari's victory.

Sure enough, he laughs harder.

"You didn't think I would let him win, did you, Granddaughter? A Warrior?" he tsks, shaking his head and gesturing for the guards to raise the gates.

The groan of the portcullis rattles my bones and echoes through the water.

He can't. Not after everything. Not this death for the man who had dreams of a better life, a life with me, one where our people were free of this monster and the depravity he inflicts upon every member of his kingdom.

Ari will not die by a beast who is bound to my family. He will not suffer one more time for his connection to me.

"No!" The word escapes me, but it falls on deaf ears. "Ari!"

It's too late, though. The dragon is already free. Her

long body circles the arena, her yellow eyes fixed on my mate as she carefully assesses him.

"Finish him," Cepheus orders, but the dragon doesn't move.

Cepheus stills. And for the first time since I have known him, his features are drawn in shock. Everything he does is intentional.

Until now.

Until the dragon he had the nerve to *own* when they were only ever meant to be free.

The dragon glances up to me and then back to Ari, before bowing her head—acknowledging him as my mate with all that implies. I feel the moment it clicks for Ari, a rightness settling over his bones as he turns to face us. His turquoise eyes churn like storms on the raging seas. Ari lifts his trident, pointing it directly at the man next to me.

"Cepheus, King of Mayim." His projecting voice fills the entire arena, making certain every single Mayima hears him. "Your dragon will not hurt me, because she recognizes me as your heir. As such, I invoke the right to formally challenge you in a fight to the death."

CHAPTER FIFTY

ARIIHAU

I hold Cepheus' gaze, not daring to look away for a moment. He can't back down from this challenge. It would make him look weak. Weaker than he already is now that the dragon has defied his orders.

The massive beast continues to circle the arena, her scales glowing almost as brightly as her eyes. A roar erupts from her mouth, rings of water following the sound.

That sound used to terrify me. But something has changed. I felt it the moment she locked eyes with me moments ago. A thrumming in my veins. A bond snapping into place.

Cepheus senses it too—how all of his power is slipping away right in front of him. That is undoubtedly the only reason why he swims down to meet me in the center of the arena.

Once he forced me into the games, his plans became all the more transparent.

This competition was never just about Melodi. Sure he

wanted someone strong on the throne, he needs an heir. But his methods also conveniently took out the rival households, further eliminating the power of his people. Giving them false hope, while in truth just strengthening his chokehold on them.

But I am done playing his games.

I still feel the ghost of his punishing grip on Melodi's throat, and the grief that flooded our bond as she watched Napo struggle to stay alive. It was the fuel I needed to push past the final leg of the battle, and the only reason I could bring myself to kill Nino.

I remind myself that there will be time to mourn the dead later, once I have added one final addition to their numbers.

"How very bold of you, Commander Ariihau," Cepheus says, taking his position right in front of me. "I suppose it will be better this way, killing you now before you sully the royal line even more than you already have."

I snarl.

"For too long, you have oppressed your people. For too long you have spilled our blood," I say, projecting the thought loudly to the crowd.

Perhaps they didn't join the rebellion. Perhaps the entire rebellion is dead. But that doesn't mean that the Mayima don't want an end to this tyranny any less than Lani did. Jopali. Nino.

Only one more person needs to die for this cause.

"That ends today, Cepheus," I continue. "It ends when we celebrate your final breath, and we rid the ocean of your tainted soul."

Cepheus is feral.

He signals for the guards to fit him with armor and bring his weapons. They hesitate briefly before obeying, and I wonder if it's his order they're unsure of, or the giant dragon that is still circling us.

From the corner of my eye, I catch sight of Melodi pulling the body of my cousin into the royal box. She ushers one of the servants over from the crowd, and they work on unbinding his hands and feet.

I send my thanks through the bond and feel her reassurance in return.

Cepheus doesn't give a warning before lunging for me. As soon as his armor is in place, he's all but shoving his guards away, charging forward like a bull shark. My muscles are strained, but adrenaline and fury keep me moving. I raise my trident just in time to block his. The impact is enough to rattle my bones, causing my arms to shake.

He rains down blow after blow with a relentless fury. The king is strong. He may use his warriors and a dragon to fight his battles when he wants to, but the rapid-fire way he's fending off these attacks is just one more reminder of how he has gotten away with his abuse of power for so long.

Only the king's heirs can challenge him, but he had many, each of them stronger than the last. And he bested every one.

He comes at me in a flurry of movements, swimming over and under me, circling me. The crowd has broken its self-imposed silence. Low murmurs and whispers drift down from the seats above us, just loud enough for me to make out the general ideas.

They talk of the end of Cepheus' reign, of possibilities for the future. They speak of hope, in a way I have never witnessed before.

Better yet, Cepheus hears them. His rage only spurs him to fight harder, though, for his pride and for his power—the only two things he has any real love for. His face contorts and twists in fury as he slices through the water again and again.

Minute after exhausting minute passes until I lose track of how long we've been fighting. The king fights with the renewed energy of someone who has been resting, waiting. Bracing himself for this very moment.

But I am bone-weary. The blood on my hands is weighing me down, and each strike rings more true than the last. It's becoming harder and harder to block, and he lands a blow against my ribcage, then my calf. My back. My arm.

I am flagging, and he knows it.

He gives me a vicious smirk when the spikes of his trident rake over my shoulder. Blood pours from the black lines of my inked skin. I barely fend off the next attack as I spin through the water, twisting through the arena like a fish on a line.

All the while, the dragon continues her frantic circling. Her eyes are wide, locked onto each of our movements.

Cepheus grins more broadly, his eyes narrowing on me like he's already won. And maybe he has.

Maybe I spoke too soon. I shouldn't have challenged him. Not yet, at least. I should have waited. I should have spoken with Melodi, made a plan.

My thoughts are a maelstrom of my mistakes, pain

muddling the world around me until all I see is everything I should have done differently. Worst of all is that Kala feels this, too. Will she feel it when I go?

She is strong enough to survive my death, though I would do anything to keep her from that kind of agony. Give anything. But I am running out of strength to give.

Peace, my love. She speaks in the deepest part of my mind in steady, soothing tones. Her voice is like warm water after swimming through an icy sea. Like a balm to each of my wounds.

Then, a wave of emotion comes crashing into me, a torrent of determination barreling through our bond. All of her love and her compassion and her endless well of faith in me flood my veins until my limbs tingle with awareness.

Before I know it, I'm pushing Cepheus back, slamming my trident against his with one arm while swinging my sword down with another. I land a hit to his thigh, and blood pools from the wound. It spirals out around him, mingling with the sea and enticing the hungry sharks above.

His lips pull back in a snarl. A hush falls over the crowd as if they can hardly believe that their king is mortal. That he can bleed like so many of his people have.

Again and again, I strike until the tides have turned, until he falters. His feet scrape the sand and he stumbles, his eyes going wide when he realizes the dragon has tightened into a circle around us. With me above him, he has nowhere to go.

A wall of scales shimmers and stretches, moving even closer than before. I strike Cepheus again, forcing him backward, toward *her*. The dragon flares her nostrils and bares her teeth, her head looming just behind him.

Another furious hit has him dropping his sword. I don't let up, I keep pushing, keep fighting, locking our tridents together and wrenching him closer. He tries to counter my blade but it's too late. It's already buried hilt-deep in his abdomen.

The king's trident slips from his grasp. Panic floods his veins, swimming in his eyes—so like his granddaughter's in their shape and color, but so devoid of her compassion and life and goodness that I don't struggle to hold his gaze.

He calls out for his warriors to save him, but even if they wanted to, they won't. He has taught them to respect strength, and right now he is weak.

His mouth drops open in fury, in shock. I can't deny a surge of satisfaction as I twist the blade before ripping it from his flesh.

A hush falls over the crowd as Cepheus sputters and bleeds all over the arena where he has killed and maimed and tortured his people for centuries. His hands go to his wound, an attempt to stop the bleeding, but it won't help.

Even if I were to show him mercy now, something he doesn't deserve, his fate has already been decided.

A shadow falls over him, and his eyes go wide. He already knows what comes next. Already feels death approaching. A grimace splits his lips, his chest rising and falling, his pulse racing faster with each second. He turns to meet his fate, and the dragon's eyes narrow. Blue flames fill her mouth and nose.

It's more than her recognition of Melodi, of me. She

finally has the freedom to punish the man who enslaved her for so long, who forced her to live in a cage and fight his battles, to maim and maul and destroy when she was only ever meant to protect.

And she is hungry for vengeance.

In one fell swoop, she brings her sharp teeth down over his body, ripping him apart, limb by limb. The sound of his cries and the crunching of bone fill the air until she severs his body in half, destroying every last remaining part of him. Cheers erupt from the crowd.

The king is dead.

CHAPTER FIFTY-ONE

ZAINA

a day has passed, and my adrenaline still hasn't faded from the twenty seconds I spent believing Madame had come for us. But there had been only a distant recognition in her amethyst gaze. No rage. No betrayal. No maternalistic disappointment.

The residual weakness in my limbs is enough to make me realize we will never be truly ready to face Madame, if she still has the power to affect us on this scale.

But then, I knew that already. Still, we have no choice.

What I wasn't prepared for, and still trying to process, is that Madame has a twin sister.

Danica is back in the water, now. She passed on what knowledge she had, along with an offer to sneak us onto shore. Einar asked her about Mayiman weapons, but she said they would be useless for us since we don't have the necessary strength to back our blows, especially since air hardens the already thick skin of the Mayima.

Danica passed along something else, too. It looks like an auger shell, but it's so much more than that. It's the only real hope we've had since the day Madame killed Remy's parents.

Now, all that's left to do is wait.

My gaze flits back down to the water, though once I spy the violet head swimming just beneath the surface, I quickly look away. Danica has been helpful, and even brought news of my sister, but it's hard to look at her.

Hard to trust her.

Hard to reconcile the pieces of the plan we've come up with since she arrived.

Hardest of all to hear her talk about her darling *Ulla* like she was a person and not just the monster who loved and grieved and destroyed the world for it. A chill rakes down my spine at the unexpected wave of understanding I felt when Danica told me Madame's story.

"You aren't like her." Einar doesn't struggle to follow the direction of my thoughts.

Perhaps the self-loathing is written all over my face.

But I think of Madame, and of the dragons. Knowing what I know now, it isn't hard to guess she needed to use them for her revenge. Didn't I threaten to do the same?

What would I have done, if I had lost my sisters? Einar?

I lean into my husband, soaking up the comfort I can never quite seem to feel deserving of.

"Am I not?" I ask. "I wasn't bluffing about the dragons."

"You would burn the world down to save the people you love, Zaina. That much is true." He tightens his arms around me. "But you wouldn't do it just to retaliate."

"Is that so different?" My voice is smaller than I mean for it to be.

"It's different enough." He speaks in what I have come to think of as his *king voice*, even and confident, with no room for argument.

I'm not sure he's right, but I let myself believe it anyway because it's better than facing the truth that I might be just as much of a monster as she is. Besides, it's not like he fools himself about how unflinchingly ruthless I can be.

He's counting on it. *Sands*, our entire plan revolves around it—the plan I wish I could stop thinking about. The scheme that we devised is brutal, requiring each of our unique skillsets and costing us something in turn. And it still might not be enough.

I run through the details relentlessly in my head, stopping only when Einar takes it upon himself to distract us both. Then I allow him to pull me down to the cabin below, taking me in his strong, steady arms and chasing both of our demons away until all we see is one another. Perhaps I should feel guilty, spending the last hours with him instead of finding another way to prepare for tonight. But we need this, to face what's coming.

To remind us what we're fighting for.

CHAPTER FIFTY-TWO

MELODI

*I*t's over.

I bring a shaking hand to my lips, my entire body going limp as I stare down at Ari. My mate. The warrior who finally defeated the king. Shock follows on the heels of my relief—not because he defeated Cepheus, but at the implications of his victory.

Ari is King. Which means that I'm not Kala anymore. I'm Queen.

Kane smiles. Whatever intense tonics Moli used on him have already taken effect. Though he is still bruised and bloody, he is conscious. And more importantly, alive. Moli packs up her tonics to escort me to Ari, who is covered in his fair share of wounds.

His cousin insists on coming, too, scooping up Napo in his shaking arms to accompany us.

My mind whirls as we make our way down to the arena where Ari stands stoically. He crosses the trench to stand at my side, speaking in the deepest part of my mind.

"Hara—well, Hara'ni, actually," he corrects, adding the honorific. "But you'll always be Kala to me."

Always.

Because we're free to be together now. Somewhere through my elation, the thought gnaws at something bittersweet inside of me. Before I can think too hard on it, another roar echoes out around us. The dragon flexes her colossal frame, shaking off the blood from her lips.

Moli and Kane hang back, though Napo tries to reach out curiously. My heart thunders in my chest as she lumbers toward us. I angle myself in between her and the others, just in case.

But she only dips her head, as though she's bowing. She's so close, I can feel the heat radiating from her mouth. Something tugs inside of me, a pull to her similar to the one I feel with Ari.

I glide forward, my hand outstretched. I place my palm on her flat nose, and she closes her eyes. Her heartbeat courses through me, and she nudges my hand, rubbing her scales against my skin. Several centuries of sadness reverberates in my chest.

"You don't have to go back to that cave ever again," I whisper. "You don't have to hurt anyone."

The dragon looks to Ari, as if to confirm my words. My mate steps closer, wrapping an arm around my back and dipping his head once. The dragon nuzzles him as well before retreating to the side of the arena, stretching like she's testing her newfound freedom.

She doesn't go far, and her yellow gaze flits protectively between us and the stunned crowd.

I turn my attention to the people at last. As one, they

make the same gesture of obeisance they made for Cepheus. It's hesitant, though, almost fearful. I understand why when a group of warriors comes forward, those my grandfather relied on the most.

They prostrate themselves before us, baring the backs of their necks and casting wary looks at the dragon.

"The honor is yours," the woman in front says.

To me? To Ari?

I look at him briefly, seeing his jaw set in a stern line. For the first time, it occurs to me what being Queen means. Not just freedom to be with Ari, but freedom to change things. To live in a world that is not fueled by violence and fear and brutality. To create that world for myself and for the people.

My people.

Feeling Ari's approval through our bond, I cross over to the warriors, placing my hand on the shoulder of the nearest one.

"Rise," I say gently, turning to address the entire group. "I don't want your lives. I want your loyalty, going forward into this new kingdom with us. I want you to help us create something better."

They look up in bewilderment, glancing from me to Ari as though they can hardly believe what they're being told.

My soulmate nods and grabs my hand, proclaiming loud enough for the arena to hear, "The honor is all of ours."

I have heard the Mayima cheer before as puppets for my grandfather's sick regime, but I have never heard the thunderous roar that greets me now.

"My king." Kane bows to Ari, a wan smile at the corner of his lips. Then he turns to me. "Shall I call you Hara'ni, or will you always be Kala to me as well?"

I shake my head, suppressing a small smile. "I'll settle for Melodi."

He dips into another bow. "Of course, Hara'ni."

Moli draws nearer to treat Ari, and warmth spreads over me at the sight of those who are rapidly becoming family to me.

Family.

Though I am hopeful about this new world of ours, I finally put my finger on the bittersweet feeling tainting the edges of this victory.

I can't move forward with one family at the cost of abandoning another. My sisters are still stuck under Mother's thumb, and so are the people of Delphine.

Maybe I'm not a fighter, but I will not stand by like a coward while they fight for their right to be free of her. Even in the light of my certainty, my stomach sinks.

Can I really leave Ari now, when we finally have a chance to be together?

You won't have to leave me, Kala. Where you go, I will go.

There is a finality in his words that wraps around me, comforting the broken, abandoned pieces of me. I believe him. We can have this. We can build a life together.

As soon as I take care of the life I left behind.

CHAPTER FIFTY-THREE

REMY

I have swallowed far more seawater than the stars ever intended for a human to ingest, but I can't deny that having Danica's help to reach the island was invaluable. Even if it's nearly impossible for me to look at her without feeling the scores of hatred I have for her sister.

We swim for miles before she deposits me on a hidden beach where the others are already waiting. She doesn't linger for drawn out goodbyes. Without a word, she dips back under the water.

It's for the best. She makes the rest of us uneasy with her eerily familiar eyes and light purple hair. It's too reminiscent of the monster we've come here to kill.

While I strip out of my wet clothes, drying off with the towel Einar has tossed my way, Aika pulls dry clothes from my pack. She also pulls out a familiar ball of orange fluff.

"Pumpkin," she quietly scolds, even as she pulls his shivering body closer to hers, tucking him into her cloak for warmth. "You were supposed to stay back with Khijhana."

That was the only drawback to this plan, that it doesn't allow the giant cat to accompany us. She couldn't swim this distance, and she is far too big for Danica to carry. In response to my wife's chiding, the monkey makes a small, simpering noise that sounds like a whining child.

I roll my eyes at them as I finish dressing. It's not like this mission isn't dangerous enough already. Now we have Aika's monkey-child to worry about as well. The damned thing had better survive.

As soon as I'm dressed, Zaina pours the contents of a dark vial onto a cloth and secures it around my neck. It's a protection in case I have to use my darling, savage wife's favorite immobilizing concoction. It's one of many safe-guards, an addition to the small emergency packs of tonics Zaina made each of us.

I thank her, and she nods in response before turning to go. She doesn't say goodbye. Neither does her husband as he follows her into the treeline where they will wait for me to complete my part of the plan.

Goodbye is not something any of us can afford to acknowledge, not when we are walking headfirst into the riskiest odds I've played yet. Our plan is far from perfect, but in a sea of bad choices, it's the only one that makes sense.

Aika finishes securing her braid, then crosses the distance to me. She leans up on her toes, pressing her lips to mine. I crush her body against me, savoring the taste of her like it's both the first and last time. Her tongue darts out to taste mine as she deepens the kiss, and for a moment, there is nothing but her.

When she pulls away, it's too soon. She gives me a cocky smirk, though her eyes tell a different story—one where she is far less flippant than she lets on.

"See you soon, Remikins." Then she winks before she literally disappears into the treeline.

She is pure shadow, an extension of her surroundings. Visceral memories of watching her in the alleyways of Bondé come back to me. The Flame. The Vigilante. The Queen. My world.

A pang shoots through my chest and I remind myself of Einar's words. There is life on the other side of this. Now, it's time to fight for it.

Securing the poisons and daggers to my sword belt, I consider the argument I had with Aika before we left the ship.

"It would be easier to just kill them." Her hands are clenched into tiny fists. "They knew what they signed up for."

I shake my head, taking a step closer to her, my hands resting on her shoulders.

"No, Aika. They could be trapped like you were. No one else needs to die because of Madame. Let's end this the right way."

Her dark eyes meet mine, softening just a little as she stretches up to wrap her arms around my neck.

"You and your infinite mercy."

It wasn't only mercy, though. Aika and Zaina explained Madame's meticulous system. Even immobilizing the guards at the back gate could cause too much attention from the others.

Which is where I come in. I stroll up like I belong there.

"Madame is expecting me," I fib easily.

That's why I'm here. Aika is too recognizable, and the other two are mediocre liars, at best. The several men on guard exchange dubious looks.

"She said not to let anyone pass," the one in front says hesitantly.

Hesitant because Madame no doubt did say that, but there isn't a trace of dishonesty in my tone.

"It must have slipped her mind. Of course, I could always leave. I'm sure she won't be too upset if she has to wait another few months for me to come back around. I mean, not with you, anyway," I add congenially. "It would hardly be your fault, after all."

The blood drains from the guard's face, and he scrambles to open the iron gate. I whistle through my teeth.

"Must be quite a boss you have there."

One guard scoffs, and another shakes his head rapidly in warning, like this is a test from Madame. It does sound like something she would do. I sigh in sympathy as I walk through the gate, then turn as though I've forgotten something.

I'm close enough to use the drug that's in my sleeve if I need to, but too far for them to attack without warning. The others are in the treeline, but if they have to intervene, our plan is already half-blown.

"She's not invincible, you know," I say quietly.

The men freeze, which is what I wanted. They're still facing me, and not the open gate.

"Yes," one of them murmurs. "She is."

Fear makes his voice reedy, but there is a question in his tone—something curiously akin to hope. And not one of them has attacked yet. In our many planning conversations, Zaina surmised that Madame would be even more volatile than usual. That even people who are oppressed and terrified reach a point where they have nothing left to lose.

These men are already halfway there. I just need to prod them in the right direction, to persuade them to keep my presence here a secret until morning and to ignore any suspicious activity they may or may not observe in the house. The ship is on the way. If we lose, they can take their families to safety on the boat before she finds them.

If we win, they can be free of her forever. I just need to convince them of that.

Three wraiths slip past the gate while the men keep their rapt attention on me. Giving them a crooked smile, I throw out my hand in a challenge. My favorite challenge, in fact.

"Would you care to wager on it?"

CHAPTER FIFTY-FOUR

ZAINA

*W*hen I walked out of Castle Alfhild to meet Damian all those months ago, I knew with an unshakable certainty that I was walking to my death. Yet I managed to face that night with more bravery than I feel right now.

Perhaps the difference is that I have more to lose.

Einar's words about a future resound in my head, all the things he wants us to have.

A life. A child. The chance to find my family—all of it is so close to being within my grasp.

We just have to get through today first.

Einar moves through the trees on surprisingly stealthy footsteps as I sneak through the courtyard. The balcony I used to share with my sisters looms above me, dark and ominous, like a stormcloud just before a twister touches down.

A lantern shines from the smaller bedroom Damian occupies on the first floor, underneath the balcony. It's another sign that despite her words, she sees him more like a guard dog than a son. Rather than grant him his own sprawling suites to match ours, she placed him where he could more easily keep an eye on us.

As if we would have dared to sneak away.

I wait until I see a shadow moving behind his window to slowly, silently ascend from his balcony to the one on the floor above. Einar is taking care of the guards around the perimeter, so no one else should be able to spot me.

In theory. It's a risk, like everything else about this plan.

Instead of going through the main doors of the balcony, I slip to the side to creep through the window that used to be mine. It isn't locked. It never needed to be. No one would have been brave enough to break in. Nor out.

Everything is just as I remember it, somehow both lavish and empty. In the corner sits the four-poster bed where I sobbed myself to sleep after Madame killed Rose. Where I wasted away night after night, coming in from my missions and my kills and endless nights of using my body as a lure for the victims she gave me.

Where Damian trapped me more than once, stopping just short of the one thing his precious *mother* might not forgive him for.

Will this feel like a victory for him?

On heavy footsteps, I make my way over to the nightstand. An ornate lantern decorates the table. Like everything else in this room, it is pristine. The oil is filled to the brim, the wick freshly cut and ready to be lit.

I expected dust, expected that Madame would let this space turn into a tomb in the year since I left. It's worse, somehow, the way she has kept it spotless like she is expecting me to come home. To her.

I slide the drawer open to find the comb she would run through my hair when I was a child. Picking it up, I run my fingers along the ivory edges, fighting back the memories that lay siege to me.

You're so beautiful, my daughter.

I can still feel the sharp spokes digging into my scalp the day she overheard me telling Rose I couldn't remember what my parents looked like.

I don't understand why you insist on being such a disappointment, Zaina, when all I've ever done is give you everything.

The comb falls to the floor with a clatter, the teeth breaking off and skittering across the polished wood panels.

I hold my breath, fighting down a curse, fighting down the panic. My heart beats an unsteady staccato in my ears, drowning out the sounds I'm straining to hear. In an effort to calm myself, I run my hand along the plush feather mattress, the gilded wooden frame, the carvings I stared at every night, wondering if I'll ever find a way to forgive Madame for the things she's done.

To forgive *myself* for the things I've done in her name.

When the door creaks open, I'm not half as startled as I should be, even knowing who is on the other side. I back against the wall, preparing for the inevitable encounter.

I have weapons, I remind myself. *I am not helpless.*

It doesn't help. I'm still breathing in harsh, uneven pants when Damian pushes the door all the way open, his eyes widening in shock.

"Sister." The word slithers across my skin, burrowing down into my bones.

Bile rises in my throat at the triumph in his gaze. I see the moment he decides not to alert Mother. After all, if she doesn't know I'm here, she can't punish him for killing me, or worse.

This is his demented dream come true.

I pull out my knife—the far less deadly of the weapons I carry—though I already know this isn't a fight I can win. All I can do now is hope that the rest of the plan goes quickly.

Because my death surely won't when Damian gets his hands on me.

CHAPTER FIFTY-FIVE

AIKA

$\mathcal{I}$'m not sure how I got stuck with what is fully the worst part of this plan when I'd much rather be privy to the merry beheading of my dear brother, but here I am, making my way toward Madame's throne room.

I should be terrified, but I've managed to lock most of that fear away in the back corners of my mind. We've already resolved to do this. Maybe we'll die today.

Then again, maybe we won't. By all rights, I should have met my end a long time ago, but I'm still here by whatever good graces the fates have for me. If I meet my end today, at least I have comfort that I will find Remy in the next life.

Or he will find me.

Voices echo off the cavernous walls before I even turn the corner. Then screams of pain and the thunk of bodies hitting the floor, the cozy backdrop of my entire life here at this chateau.

Apparently some brave soul was stupid enough to bring her word that there's been an incident.

I shake my head. That's a beginner's mistake. It's always better to let her notice an issue for herself while you're already actively taking care of it.

Then again, I'm hardly one to talk about stupid decisions as I step directly in the path of her guards. I go for my stars, taking out the first and second before they can react.

The third cries out in warning, bringing more soldiers our way. Far more. More than I was expecting, by a long shot. Did she bolster her guard when the Mayima took Mel? Did she fear retaliation?

Or did she know we were coming?

Tendrils of fear creep along my spine, in spite of myself, but I don't let them overtake me.

I take the third guard out mostly for spite because I'm not half as nice as Remy is, then fell several more before they finally manage to subdue me.

Mother dearest would be proud, if she wasn't going to be so furious.

The guards don't kill me, of course, since they don't want Madame to kill them in turn. They don't even attempt to take my satchel and check it for weapons. Which is a relief, since they would find a tiny orange monkey with big brown eyes inside.

Instead they throw open the doors and drag me to a far worse fate than death.

The blood drains from my face when I hear the familiar clacking of her fingernails against the gilded arms of her chair. I focus on the unsteady staccato of my heart as I reluctantly raise my eyes to meet hers.

She is thinner than when I saw her last, the lines of her face sharp and more angular than I remember them. Though I would never go so far as to call her frail, it's almost as though something has fractured within her. My heartbeat falters, a familiar surge of guilt at the reason I'm here even as I remember all the things she's done to deserve this.

"Daughter." The word is cold, as much a curse as a greeting. "Surely you didn't think you had a chance at besting me after the losses you sustained last time." Her words are more sharp than my silver stars, and with even less remorse. "So I can only assume you've come for your punishment?"

There are so many things I want to ask her, to say to her, but each of them dies on my lips. That's not why I'm here, and only one thing matters now.

"You can punish me later." Here's hoping that turns out to be a lie. "But right now, you need to save Zaina."

CHAPTER FIFTY-SIX

EINAR

I despise this plan nearly as much as I despise myself for making it.

Though I might hate Remy the most for planting the seeds that brought it inevitably into my mind. Even now, I know that isn't fair. All he did was raise a simple question.

Does Madame play favorites?

The rest of it had snowballed from there into a debate about how far she would take that favoritism, and how we would capitalize on that.

Though I hated the moment I looked around that table and realized I could already see the chess pieces in motion, I cannot deny that it might just give us our only real chance at victory.

At a cost we will never get back.

The plan started with Remy talking our way into the gates, then staying to be sure the soldiers didn't turn on us. That was his price. Remaining behind rather than confront the beast he came to slay, while his wife went ahead into battle.

Then there was Aika—the consummate liar.

She was the only one of us who Ulla wouldn't kill on sight, who could convince her to leave the most protected room in her house. Aika's job is arguably the most dangerous, with the highest margin for error, but she didn't so much as tremble when she left.

Even her best lies won't be enough, though, if she can't put Ulla off her guard. That's where my wife came in—the beautiful, brilliant distraction.

I don't like any part of this plan, but Zaina's role is the part I hate myself for the most. If her price is willingly baiting the psychopath who has put his hands on her more than once before, then mine is standing back while she does it.

But this is the only way through I could see.

So I did my part, taking out the excess of guards one by one while I stood near enough to intervene in case we're wrong about Ulla's reaction. Or in case something delays them. I try not to think too hard about what that might be.

If we lose Aika, I know in my soul that I will lose Zaina, too, one way or the other.

A crash sounds from the direction of the balcony. I knock the guard nearest to me out with the flat side of my axe, then quickly scale the railing to the second floor.

It takes everything I have to stay out of sight when all I want to do is run my fist through the window and use the shards to remove Damian's head from his despicable body. He is towering over Zaina, taunting her where she has taken a defensive stance against the wall. Though she has her head held high, there is real fear in her eyes.

Rage pulses through me, drowning out all of my more rational thoughts. He lunges for her, and she dodges, but it won't be enough. At some point, he will have his hands on her.

I mentally repeat every promise I made to her not to interfere, chanting them in my head like a mantra. It's the only thing staying my hand.

Then he grabs a fistful of her hair, using it to tug her against him, and I see red.

Just as I am about to set everything we have worked so hard for on fire in spite of all of my better judgment, the door slams open, crashing into the wall behind it.

And in the doorway, wearing the most furious expression I've ever seen on her, stands Ulla.

CHAPTER FIFTY-SEVEN

ZAINA

*M*adame is here.

Madame has come for me—to protect me, or to punish me, I can't be sure until her hand wraps around Damian's throat. I swallow, hard.

She has come to save me. And I have come to kill her.

I move away from the wall as she slams him against it. Madame is something feral, her lips curled up, exposing her bared teeth. She is more unhinged than I have ever seen her, and I want so badly not to recognize that any of that is on my behalf.

Though we needed this plan to work, I realize now that part of me wanted us to be wrong. I wanted anything that kept me from this sick, twisted feeling as I wait for my opportunity to use the only weapon we have against her.

Khijhana's tooth is deceptively light in my pocket. Such a small thing to fell a giant. Madame doesn't put her back to me, though, doesn't give me a single opening for me to risk going for the weapon.

"What have you done?" she snarls.

For a moment, I think she's speaking to me, but then her hand tightens around Damian's neck even more.

He chokes out words like *never* and *loyal* and *Mother*, but she is undeterred.

"You knew what I went through looking for Melodi," she emphasizes my sister's name as she slams his head against the wall again. "I have already lost one daughter, and now you try to take the ones who return to me?"

She eases up her grip just enough to let him speak.

"You don't need them." Damian's black eyes are wild, desperate. He wraps his hands around the one she has on his neck, his tone pleading as he continues speaking. "I am your loyal child. We would have gotten Melodi—"

She squeezes harder, and I wait for her to order him to the dungeons. I wait for him to go like the perverse whipped dog that he is.

But I am utterly unprepared when she takes a carefully sharpened fingernail and drags it up his sternum, splitting him from navel to neck.

She lets him drop to the floor. His eyes are wide with disbelief, with betrayal, with pain. Aika stands in the doorway, two guards slack jawed in the hall behind her. She eyes Damian with nothing but satisfaction on her features.

I should feel the same. I know I should.

Instead, I remember the day Madame brought him here, a broken, bleeding boy. Abandoned by everyone, destroyed by his father, gazing up at her with reverence in his eyes. It seems such a waste, the life of cruelty he's lived.

I'm not sad that he's dead. But neither can I find the vengeance I was expecting to feel when he loses his life at the hands of the only person he loved.

Blood pools near my feet, and I deftly step away from it, bringing my eyes up to meet Madame's.

"Come, Zaina." Her tone is eerily placid, but a muscle twitches in her jaw. "We'll discuss your discipline along with your sister's."

I stay rooted to the spot.

This is our only chance. When she leaves this room, she will likely strip us of our weapons. We will lose the only opportunity to end this.

Aika moves farther into the room, but Madame holds up a bloody hand. My sister halts in her tracks. Pumpkin slips out of the small bag she carries, scurrying to the floor. He cowers behind my sister, huddled into her skirts where he is out of Madame's sight.

If the guards notice, they don't comment.

"Rebellion, even now, Daughter?" Madame turns slowly, walking a circle around the room. "I knew you must be planning something, but surely there's more to it than this."

Her back isn't entirely toward me, but it's close enough. I gently ease my hand into my pocket. But she stops at the window to the balcony, cocking her head and inhaling sharply.

Before I can react, before I can move, she darts her arm through the glass. My lips part, a scream wrenching from my throat as she drags Einar in through the broken shards.

Shards of glass fall off of her like beads of water. Her skin is untouched, but Einar is already coated in blood.

I tell myself she won't kill him. She needs him. But her chest heaves as she looks from him to me, and I know there is no reason left in her anymore.

Before anyone can react, before I can even scream again, she takes a shard of glass and stabs it straight into my husband's chest.

CHAPTER FIFTY-EIGHT

ZAINA

*N*o. I don't know if I scream the word out loud or in my head as I lunge for Einar.

I can still fix this. I have tonics. I prepared for injuries. All I need is to reach him.

Madame drops his body and yanks me away like I hold no more weight than an insect, and I stumble to my knees in a pool of blood.

Damian's. Einar's. It swirls together on the ground, soaking into my pants and coating me in a feeling of wrongness so strong I heave the contents of my stomach. It doesn't make sense.

Einar.

My Einar.

The strong, massive, beast of a man, my solid, unyielding mountain, lying prone in a growing pool of crimson. His eyes are unfocused, but they still find mine.

"Zaina." His fingers spasm without his consent, and I stare, transfixed at the motion.

It's wrong. Those are the hands that trailed along my skin and worshiped me and held me and made me feel whole again. He is always sure of their placement, always steady in their control.

"Please," I say to Madame, not getting up from my knees. "I will do anything. I will come home, and we can be a family, and I'll never leave you again."

She looks down at me with disappointment, making a chiding noise in the back of her throat. She has a vise grip around the hand I need to access the makeshift dagger. I try to snake my other hand around, but she grabs that arm too until she holds both of my wrists in her inhumanly strong grasp, blocking my view of my dying husband.

"I gave you everything, Zaina. A throne. A family." Her voice is quiet and deadly cold, not a trace of humanity left within it. "Everything you are is because of me, but you can't appreciate it. We can never truly be a family as long as he lives."

"Yes, we can," I say, and I'm not lying. There is nothing I wouldn't do to save him. "We can be a family, and I'll find a way to get you the dragons. Anything."

Something flashes in her eyes, and I wonder if she'll cave. I need her to. If saving Einar means being the monster she wants me to be, I will do it. I will do whatever she asks.

"There will be time enough for that later, my daughter. For now, I've lost too many children as it is." She looks at Damian's corpse with what might be remorse, though it certainly isn't grief.

Broken, anguished sobs echo off the walls of this room that has only ever known despair, and it takes me too long to realize they're coming from me. Aika is turned away from me, kneeling on the ground as well. She's huddled, facing the wall like she can't bear the sight of any of this.

Of course she can't.

Because we've lost. And I've lost everything.

Einar is dying and Aika will be enslaved to Madame once more and Mel is gone.

It feels like my soul itself is tearing apart, like I have a wound in my chest that matches his, only mine will fester for eternity after he's gone. I struggle against Madame's iron grasp, but it does no good.

"Honestly, Zaina, that's enough," she says with exasperation. "Come, Aika."

Then she's dragging me away from my husband for the final time, ignoring the string of pleas and begging and bargaining coming from my lips.

Somewhere in the back of my mind, I've been counting down the seconds, tallying every ounce of blood that flows toward me on the floor. Einar is strong, but even he is not invincible. Even if it felt that way, sometimes.

His time is almost up. I have failed, and we have lost.

I'm so busy desperately studying the stream of red that I don't immediately notice the way Madame freezes, her sharp intake of air. A shadow falls over us and slowly, I lift my head to see what has utterly captivated her.

The sight is so ethereal that I wonder if I'm hallucinating. My younger sister stands bathed in a halo of light from the hallway, her deep red curls still damp from the sea, her body clothed in a gown made of turquoise netting and golden shells.

Her eyes are even warmer than I remember, filled with a compassion I couldn't have concocted in my head.

Madame confirms it when she finally speaks, her voice soft and reverential and almost human again.

"Melodi."

CHAPTER FIFTY-NINE

MELODI

I take one step forward, then another.

The room is silent, as silent as I have been for every day of my life on land. Each set of eyes are locked onto me as I push forward. The man who led me here, Remy, hisses out a breath as he takes in the sight of Aika cowering in a pool of blood. I can't tell yet if any of it belongs to her.

Panic pulses through me on a never-ending loop as I look from her to the rest of the carnage in the room before honing in on the death-grip Mother has around Zaina's wrists.

For a change, my mother's gaze is singularly fixed on me.

She stares, her violet eyes widening. An array of emotions flits through her features—a kaleidoscope of relief, anger, fear, and something else. Something like recognition.

Can she sense the bond that I've sealed. Does she know that I stand before her as a queen? A Hara?

Water drips from my gown, mingling with the blood on the floor. There is a trail leading from Damian's body in the corner all the way over to Mother. Her fingers are covered in it.

Another line of blood leads from behind her to the Jokithan King. His life is pooling out from beneath his leather armor, dripping down onto Zaina's beautiful bedroom floor.

So much death. So much bloodshed, like I have left one arena for another.

I reach out toward her with the tendrils of my thoughts, but they have nowhere to land. Is it because we are out of the water, or is it that whatever she did to make herself human cut off this side of her?

Shaking my head, I reach up and tug at the shell necklace that I have worn every single day since she first gave it to me. Mother's expression flickers, but she doesn't loosen her grasp.

He wouldn't have wanted this for you, I think at her, willing her to understand my intent.

Another step forward, and finally, I'm standing right in front of her. I glance pointedly from her face down to the necklace, thinking about the memory that Danica shared with me. Can she remember the part of her who loved and hoped and danced long enough to let my sister go? To stop from destroying the lives of the children she claimed for herself?

You know what they are to each other. This time I look from Zaina to her dying husband. *And you know what this will do to her if he dies.*

My mother may not be able to hear my thoughts, but

comprehension flickers over her features. She stretches out the hand not restraining my sister, moving it almost subconsciously toward the conch shell. Unexpected tears fill her eyes as I place the necklace in her trembling, blood-stained fingers.

For all of the destruction and death she has wrought, this is something she has that her father didn't. A heart—small and broken, covered in decay and filled with ruination, but it beats for the people she loves.

Even if that love is as twisted as she is.

Movement catches my eye as I watch my mother's elegant fingers trace the shell, following the grooves in a familiar rhythm.

I know what comes next.

And even though it breaks something inside of me, even though I know I'm losing something I will never get back, I also know that I can't stop it. I won't.

Isn't that why I came?

CHAPTER SIXTY

AIKA

*E*very stilted heartbeat reverberates through me, echoing in my mind. They thrum through my veins, drumming a slow and steady beat as I stand.

Melodi holds Madame's gaze, but I know she sees me, that she knows what I'm about to do. Grief flits through her eyes for a fraction of a moment, but acceptance is on its heels.

That feels worse, somehow, tugging at the strings of the guilt that already threatens to tear me apart.

But even if this wasn't what we came here to do, I've made my choice. My sister's sobs still permeate every inch of this space, sounds I have never heard her make before. It's just a small piece of the suffering Madame inflicts everywhere she goes.

So I creep closer.

Zaina turns, my movements tearing her attention away from Einar. Her expression is horrified until she realizes what's in my hands. Her fingers graze the pocket of her gown, searching for the makeshift blade that isn't there.

Pumpkin wraps his body around my ankle, clinging to me for dear life. He's been hiding there since I urged him to fetch me the tooth.

I raise my clenched fist, looking to both of my sisters one final time. For permission? For forgiveness? I can't be sure.

Either way, I know that this ends today. Then my eyes meet Remy's. One final look, in case this doesn't work.

When Madame steps closer to Mel, bringing a hand up to caress her face, I set on fire what's left of my soul to take advantage of her distraction, her rare moment of humanity.

Then I bring the dagger down with every last ounce of strength I possess.

There's a choking sound, and she spins, betrayal in her amethyst gaze. In a lightning fast movement, she pulls the tooth out from her back, looking from it to me with an expression that morphs closer and closer to fury.

"Still not good enough, Aika." She throws out an arm, backhanding me against the wall then stalking toward me.

Stars line my vision, and I can't breathe. Everything happens at once.

Remy races toward me. Mel reaches out to stop Madame, and Zaina is getting to her feet, but I know it won't be enough if we were wrong.

I have less than a second to worry that it hasn't worked, that the final piece of our plan was a failure, or perhaps a trick from a woman who wasn't ready to let her sister die.

Then Madame falters.

"Wha—" she cuts off, horror dawning on her features. "Poison."

A bitter huff of air escapes her lips, followed by a thin rivulet of blood.

The auger shell that Danica had given us was filled with just enough poison to coat Khijhana's tooth. It was the closest we could come to a guarantee—all we had to do was nick her skin.

Remy reaches my side, and Zaina slides across the bloodsoaked floor to get to Einar, wasting not even the time it will take her to watch this death unfold. I half-expect Madame to keep going, to try to get her revenge in her final moments even though we both know it would be in vain.

Instead, she turns back to Melodi, her hand still clutching the conch shell in a spasming, weakening grasp. Then she stumbles forward.

My younger sister reaches out to catch her mother.

Somewhere in the background, I hear Zaina's frantic muttering, see her shaking fingers taking out vial after vial from Einar's belt and forcing them down his throat, pouring some directly on his wounds.

Remy checks me for injuries before going to help my sister, holding Einar's wound closed while Zaina works.

I should help, too. But all I can seem to do is stare at the only mother I have ever known. She was a monster and she was a person and I'm not sure which of those things feels worse right now.

Mel's grip on Madame slips, and they fall to the floor.

Tears stream down her face, falling to mingle with the

blood that seems to coat every surface of this room as she pulls Madame's head into her lap. Then she gently takes the necklace she had held out mere moments ago and fastens it around her mother's neck.

"You really are entirely his," she says, her voice little more than a whisper. "Entirely my Makani's."

A cough wrenches out of her and she shudders once, then twice, before going completely still. Only then do I finally find the strength to move, to cross the short distance to her. Sinking down to my knees, I reach out with trembling fingers to close her eyelids.

For Mel's sake, I tell myself.

Not because I can't stand the sightless purple orbs, devoid of life, devoid of the hatred that burned from their depths, devoid of the rare moments of approval she was capable of showing.

Devoid of everything.

It's such a quiet ending for a woman who did so much, so much less than she deserved, but so much more than I ever thought we would be capable of.

Finally, I get to my feet, but not before I whisper the goodbye that we never thought would come.

CHAPTER SIXTY-ONE

ZAINA

*T*he sun is just creeping over the horizon when my sisters and I stand outside of the place we spent more than half of our lives imprisoned.

It seems impossible that everything has happened in one night. That Einar survived.

He sits behind me, resting against Khijhana, who arrived with the boat, still angry with me that she had been left behind.

Melodi has just returned from telling her mate that she was all right. Or at least, physically unharmed. It doesn't feel like any of us are all right. I'm not sure we ever will be.

He waits in the water nearby, watching Mel with the same intensity I have come to expect from Einar.

Not that Remy is much better with Aika. He just hides it in a way the other two don't bother to. He stands behind Aika, suffering stoically through the curious attentions of a large purple octopus.

All of our eyes are trained on the house, though.

I already walked the halls, feeling Rose's ghost alongside me as I plucked the vials I needed from Madame's storeroom. As Melodi prepared her body in a way I'm not sure she deserved. As Aika meticulously created a trail of turpentine along the floor, and another around the perimeter.

We'll never have the answers we so desperately need. They died right alongside her, but at least it's over. There's only one thing left to do now, to drive the final nail in her coffin.

"Whenever you're ready," I say to my sisters.

"We've been ready," Aika mutters. "Just waiting on you to have your whole dramatic moment."

She says it casually, but her words are edged with a bittersweet tone that I feel inside my soul.

This house was a prison, but it was also the only real home we knew—the place where Madame took one family from me and gave me another.

"Says the woman who had this idea to begin with," I shoot back.

Mel shakes her head softly, fondly, but she makes a gesture for us to move on.

"All right then," I say, my voice wavering slightly with disbelief.

Aika holds out a vial and hands out three small matches. One by one, we dip our matches into the vial and smoke and sparks burst to life.

We drop them to the ground.

Then we stand back and watch the life Madame forced on us go up in flames.

EPILOGUE

Melodi

I haven't returned to Delphine in the year since my sisters and I burned the chateau to the ground. I probably never will, but my people bring back reports that the villagers on the isle are doing well, trying to rebuild after Mother's reign of terror.

Aren't we all?

Most days, this newfound freedom still doesn't quite feel real. The nights are even worse. I wake up in a cold sweat, remembering Damian's hands on me, the way I had accepted a fate that would have slowly destroyed me.

Then I see my mother die all over again, feel the life she wasted on hatred draining away in my hands.

All we can do is move forward, Kala, Ari says to me in those precarious in-between hours.

He's right. We can only do better, create better for our own people, just as my sisters are doing for theirs.

Like I've summoned them with my thoughts, Aika and Zaina walk through the double doors at the back of the cabin, joining the rest of us outside. Shortly after Delphine, we came here and built a place of our own on the beach at the intersection between our three kingdoms.

It runs right into the surf at the edge so Ari and I can stay as well, though I'm not sure it's a gesture he appreciates when Aika spends our time together mocking him.

"How's our favorite grumptopus today?" she asks, looking pointedly at my husband rather than the actual grumpy octopus winding around a stool next to her.

My grin stretches wide and Ari sighs.

"Really, Kala?" he asks, pulling me into his arms. "You take her side, even now?"

He presses a kiss to my temple and I shrug like I don't feel fire building everywhere he touches. Sighing, he rests his chin on my head and looks to Remy for help next.

Remy only laughs, of course, pulling my middle sister onto his lap and telling her not to taunt the giant merman. She chuckles, too, though it is as shadowed as the rest of ours.

She has never said how she felt about being the one to kill Mother, and I will never ask her. I'm not sure I want to know if she felt guilty or vindicated or sad.

I'm not sure it's my place to ask when she did what the rest of us couldn't.

"Aika," Zaina begins to chide, but Einar cuts her off with a head shake.

Aika smirks. "Grandpa doesn't want my attention on him instead."

"Yet here you grace me with it," Einar responds with a long-suffering sigh of his own.

"How else would I distract you?" she says.

He raises his eyebrows and she tilts her head toward where her tiny monkey is holding out Einar's ring, making a sound that is suspiciously close to laughter.

Zaina has given up, lounging against her enormous cat and ignoring them all.

I bite back a smile, though it fades when I see the worried way my oldest sister runs her hand back and forth across her swelling belly. Einar, too, tracks the movement, concern in his gaze.

Not for the babe, which appears to be growing just fine, but for Zaina, who can't seem to believe that Mother won't pop out of the shadows to take everything she loves from her.

Not that I blame her.

I feel that way, too, every time I look at Ari, at my sisters, at the pieces of life we have been granted against all of the odds. We aren't quite living happily ever after, yet. But we are here, together. We survived.

Most of us, anyway.

Roses climb the side of the house as a reminder for the one we lost. There are no memorials to Mother or Damian, but we remember our sweet sister in a way we were never allowed to before.

Aika pulls out her fiddle, looking at Zaina with a challenge. My oldest sister rolls her eyes, but gets to her feet with far more grace than anyone in her condition should be able to. She glides over to the piano that rests just inside the double doors and sits down, playing in time to Aika's music.

They play, and I dance, and it's a bittersweet sensation of both being surrounded by the ghosts of our past and finding a way to leave them where they belong.

So no, it isn't happily ever after. But it's close enough for now.

A MESSAGE FROM US

We need your help!

Did you know that authors, in particular indie authors like us, make their living on reviews? If you enjoyed this book, please take a moment to let people know on all of the major review platforms like; Amazon, Goodreads, and/or Bookbub!

(Social Media gushing is also highly encouraged!)

Remember, reviews don't have to be long. It can be as simple as whatever star rating you feel comfortable with and an: 'I loved it!' or: 'Not my cup of tea...'

Now that that's out of the way, if you want to come shenanigate with us, rant and rave about these books and others, get access to awesome giveaways, exclusive content and some pretty ridiculous live videos, come join us on Facebook at our group, Drifters and Wanderers

You can also get a FREE copy of our standalone

Thumbelina retelling, plus stay up to date on all our bookish news by joining our newsletter here: mahleand madison.com/newsletter

If you're desperate for more ElBin Books, you can click here for a sneak peek at our bestselling enemies-to-lovers fantasy romance, Scarlet Princess.

Pronunciation Guide

Zaina	zī-EEN-ah
Einar	Āy-nar
Khijhana	kee-JAUN-ah
Chalyx	CHAL-ix
Corentin	COR-en-tin
Aika	Ī-eek-ah
Madame	Mah-DAUM
Ulla	OO-lah
Bondé	BON-day
Kala	KAHL-ah
Ariihau	AHR-ee-how
Cepheus	SEF-ee-us
Mayim	MY-eem
Mayima	my-EEM-ah
Napo	NAH-poe

ELBIN'S ACKNOWLEDGMENTS

There are so many people to thank with every book, but even more so at the end of a series...let alone one as demanding as this one!

First and foremost, we want to thank our beta readers. Without Lissa, this series would have started out pretentious and boring. And without the rest of you, it would have ended that way, too.

Michelle Fritz, thank you so much for all your hard work and your last minute help on this project. Without this, we never would have gotten this book done on time. <3

Emily, the keeper of our lives and the organizer of our souls, we adore you and appreciate you more than we ever say!

To all of our Book Biscuits, our Drifters and Wanderers, and everyone who has supported us by reading, reviewing, sharing, and just coming to hang out with us, you are the literal reason we keep doing what we do. There would be no ElBin without you, and certainly no Of Songs and Silence.

To Jesikah Glorious-Potato-Fairy Sundin, you are the feather in our caps, the light of our lives, the wind beneath our wings...but we digress. Just like every underwater cavern needs a hammerhead of love, we need you in our lives, and this book certainly needed you in its life.

And finally, to our families, who put up with us during this entire long process. Thank you for dealing with our second-hand sadness as we agonized with these characters, with our insane deadlines as we wrangled them into shape, and with our general personalities as we...existed.

We love you all. <3

ABOUT THE AUTHORS

Elle and Robin can usually be found on road trips around the US haunting taco-festivals and taking selfies with unsuspecting Spice Girls impersonators.

They have a combined PH.D in Faery Folklore and keep a romance advice column under a British pen-name for raccoons. They have a rare blood type made up solely of red wine and can only write books while under the influence of the full moon.

Between the two of them they've created a small army of insatiable humans and when not wrangling them into their cages, they can be seen dancing jigs and sacrificing brownie batter to the pits of their stomachs.

And somewhere between their busy schedules, they still find time to create words and put them into books.

ALSO BY ELLE & ROBIN

The Lochlann Treaty Series:

Winter's Captive

Spring's Rising

Summer's Rebellion

Autumn's Reign

The Lochlann Feuds Series:

Scarlet Princess

Tarnished Crown

Crimson Kingdom

Obsidian Throne

The Lochlann Deception Series:

Hollow Court

Fragile Oath

The World Apart Series By Robin D. Mahle:

The Fractured Empire

The Tempest Sea

The Forgotten World

The Ever Falls

Unfabled Series:

Promises and Pixie Dust

Made in United States
Orlando, FL
05 January 2024

42146591R00200